Professor P

and the

Jurassic Coast

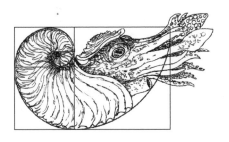

Best wishes

Peter J Davidson

About the author

I was born in London in 1957 and studied Theoretical Physics at Corpus Christi College, Cambridge. After leaving University I began my work as an inventor, designing electronic and computer systems.

I now live in the West Country with my wife, son and our two cats. *Professor P and the Jurassic Coast* is my first children's book.

About the illustrator

Professor P

and the

Jurassic Coast

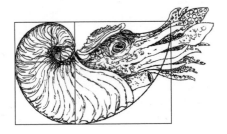

P. J. Davidson

Illustrated by

A. T. Royce

POSITIVE

BOOKS

First published in Great Britain in 2004 by:

Positive Books Limited
66 High Street, Glastonbury BA6 9DZ
info@ positive-books.co.uk
www.positive-books.co.uk

A CIP catalogue record of this book is available from
the British Library.

ISBN 0 9546151 0 7

Text printed on Corona Offset 100% recycled paper
by Barnwell's Print Ltd, Norfolk.

For my son, David.

Contents

	Prologue	1
1	The Jurassic Coast	2
2	Professor P	9
3	Inventions	18
4	The Fossil Shop	30
5	Gold	37
6	The Basement	46
7	The Safe	56
8	The Cave	64
9	Superbrain	71
10	Preparations	80
11	Help!	90
12	Quantum Mechanics	98
13	Prehistoric Island	108
14	The Raft	116
15	Shark Attack!	122
16	Reunited	129
17	The Tree House	138
18	Dinosaur!	146
19	Leaving	156
20	Home?	163
21	Alternative Worlds	172
22	Cambridge	181
23	Professor P?	187
24	Cliff Hanger	195
25	The Exhibition	204
26	Party!	211
	Fossil Guide	219

Prologue

Cambridge
Evening Post

Monday, December 2, 20

COLLEGE EXPLOSION

A huge explosion destroyed part of an historic Cambridge college today. Miraculously no one was seriously hurt.

"I was thrown to the ground by the blast," a student told our reporter. "There was purple smoke everywhere."

The cause of the explosion is still unknown but it is believed to have come from a room belonging to Professor P, a fellow of the college. He was experimenting with a new and untested form of energy.

Professor P

CHAPTER ONE

The Jurassic Coast

"Come on, Sparky!" I called as I ran onto the beach.

Sparky, my Labrador puppy, was still in the car park, nose to the ground, his little tail wagging in excitement. He scrambled down the steps and jumped onto the soft golden sand. The beach was crowded with sunbathers and the sea full of people surfing and splashing in the waves.

"Let's go exploring, Sparky. Race you to those cliffs over there!" We ran across the sand, onto the pebbles and over to the large rocks at the base of the cliffs. In front of us was a sign that read:

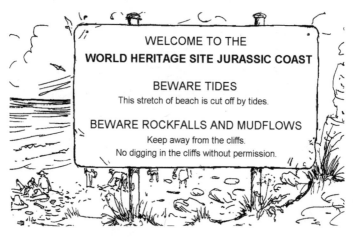

I looked up at the tall cliffs. They were made of a soft crumbly stone, light grey in colour, with darker streaks running through them. A man was standing at the base of the cliffs hitting the rocks with a hammer. I walked along the pebbles past some children playing in the rock pools.

Sparky ran over to the sea. This was the first time he had been to the seaside and he barked when a wave crashed onto the beach and splashed him.

"It's OK, Sparky, it won't hurt you!" I said, laughing at the look of surprise on his face.

Sparky shook himself, looked at me and then plunged back into the water. He swam around in circles and then ran back onto the beach. He came over to me and wagged his tail proudly as if to say, "Look at me – I can swim!" He shook himself vigorously, spraying me with water!

"Oh, Sparky! I'm soaked!" I cried.

I bent down to wipe the water off my legs. When I looked up Sparky had gone. He had run over to some rocks at the base of the cliffs and was nosing in someone's bag.

"Sparky, stop that," I shouted, racing towards him. "Come here!"

A girl looked up. She had long fair hair and was wearing a bright T-shirt with a rainbow on it.

"Sorry," I said, pulling Sparky out of her bag.

"That's all right," the girl said, smiling. "He was probably after my sandwiches."

She stroked him gently. Sparky wagged his tail and licked her hand.

"He's a lovely puppy. What's he called?"

"Sparky," I replied, "and my name's Peter."

"Hi, I'm Tara."

Sparky went over to Tara's bag and sniffed it again. As I gently pushed him away I noticed a collection of small broken stones lying next to her bag.

"What are you doing, Tara?" I asked, looking curiously at the pile of fragments.

"Looking for fossils," she replied. "Here, have a look."

Tara reached into her bag and handed me a small stone. I turned the fossil over in my hand and examined it carefully. It looked like a large snail with a spiral pattern on

3

the shell.

"What is it?" I asked, puzzled.

"It's an ammonite," she replied. "They used to live in the sea around here, millions of years ago. Their shells turn into stone and make the fossils."

"Here's another," Tara said, giving me a pencil-shaped stone.

"Looks like a large hedgehog spine," I said, looking at it curiously. "Big hedgehog though," I added jokingly.

Tara laughed. "I'm not sure what they are but there's a lot on the beach around here."

"Have you ever found a dinosaur fossil?" I asked, fascinated by these strange stones.

"Not yet," Tara replied. "But I did find a shark's tooth once!"

"A shark tooth!"

"Yes, and it was this big!" she said, holding her thumb and first finger about two centimetres apart. "It was really sharp. I found it in one of the rock pools over there."

"Do sharks still live in the sea here?" I asked.

"No," Tara replied. "Not any more. The tooth I found was millions of years old."

"Well, that's a relief!" I laughed.

"It's great fun looking for fossils," Tara continued. "You never know what you're going to discover."

"Are they easy to find?" I asked.

"Yes," she nodded. "There are lots here on the Jurassic Coast – it's a really famous place for finding fossils. People come from all over the world to look for them. Do you want to try?"

"OK," I replied enthusiastically.

Tara gave me a small grey stone. "You have to break the stones open to get the fossil out," she said, putting the stone on a large flat rock. "Then you need to hit it with this." She handed me a piece of pointed flint. "But not too hard," she warned, "or you'll smash the fossil."

I hit the little grey stone gently and it broke into three pieces. We carefully examined them.

"Nothing," Tara said. "It's often like that. You just have to keep trying."

I found another grey rock and hit it hard with the piece of flint. A little piece of the rock broke away to reveal part of a fossil.

"I think I've found one!" I cried excitedly.

"You have!" Tara said. "Be careful not to damage it."

I hammered the rock and chipped away small pieces of it until the whole fossil was revealed. It fitted snugly into the palm of my hand.

"It's a good one," Tara said, her brown eyes shining in delight.

It was great fun looking for fossils with Tara. Sparky tried to help us by splashing into all the rock pools and scrabbling at the stones with his paws. He looked on curiously as we broke the stones apart to find the fossils.

After a few hours we had collected a small pile of ammonites, lots of the 'hedgehog spines' and some fossil shells.

"I need a rest now," Tara said, wiping her brow. "I'm hungry."

She sat down on a large rock, opened her bag and took out a yellow lunch-box.

"Have you got any lunch, Peter?" she asked.

"No," I replied. "I was going to buy some sandwiches in the village."

"You can share mine if you like," she said kindly, "save you going to the shops. I've got plenty."

"Thanks," I said, sitting down beside her.

Tara gave me a sandwich and an apple and poured some

water into a cup for Sparky.

"I love looking for fossils," she said, munching on a pear. "I used to come here fossil hunting with my dad all the time when we were on holiday."

"Aren't you on holiday now?" I asked.

"No. I live here," she replied happily. "We moved a few weeks ago."

"I live here too," I said excitedly. "We moved today – to Seaview Close, on the new housing estate by the caravan park."

"That's where I live!" Tara exclaimed in surprise. "I'm really glad we moved. We used to live inland about twenty miles away. Where have you come from, Peter?"

"London," I replied. "I've never even been here before, until today.

"You'll really like it," Tara said, smiling. "It's great living by the sea. Do you like surfing?"

"I don't know," I replied. "I've never tried."

"Oh, it's great fun!" Tara said, jumping up. "I've got a spare board – do you want to borrow it?"

"OK," I replied. "Come on, Sparky, we're going surfing!"

We quickly tidied away our lunch things, packed the fossils carefully into Tara's bag and raced back along the beach. We had almost reached the large Jurassic Coast sign at the end of the cliffs when there was a sudden loud bang. Sparky barked in surprise and startled seagulls flew away from the cliffs.

"What was that?" I said in surprise.

"It sounded like an explosion," Tara replied. "I think it came from up there," she added, pointing to the cliffs.

"Let's go and see!" I said, running towards some steps.

Tara and I climbed up the steps in the cliff. Sparky scrambled up after us. When we got to the top I stopped to catch my breath and look around.

"That's odd," I said, panting. "There's no sign of an explosion."

"Where do you think it came from?" Tara asked, gazing out over the open fields.

"There!" I shouted, pointing to a small wood in the distance. "Look, smoke! Coming up out of those trees."

We ran along the footpath and down the hill towards the trees. As we got closer I could see the smoke more clearly.

"The smoke," I cried in amazement. "It's purple!"

CHAPTER TWO

Professor P

We ran down the hill towards the smoke. When we reached the wood Sparky growled suspiciously.

"What a horrid smell!" Tara said, coughing. "Do you think it's safe?"

"I don't know," I said, unsure. The strange smoke stung my eyes and was making them water. "Maybe we should wait for it to clear."

The purple smoke had settled in the trees like a heavy mist. We waited for it to disappear and after a few minutes a gust of wind blew away the last few wisps of smoke. Sparky ran ahead and soon disappeared into the thick undergrowth. We followed him through the trees until we came to a high stone wall covered in moss.

"I think the smoke came from behind this wall," I said as we stopped. Tara nodded in agreement.

The wall was too high for us to climb over so we ran along it, looking for a way through. We found an old gate covered in brambles and pushed hard against it.

"It's no use," I said disappointedly. "It won't budge. It must be bolted from the inside."

We ran along by the wall, looking for another way in. Soon we came across a large apple tree that had a branch resting conveniently on the wall.

"Tara, will you give me a leg up so I can climb onto that branch and over the wall?" I asked.

"OK," she replied. "I'll wait here with Sparky. When you get over, unbolt the gate and let us through."

Tara helped me onto the lowest branch of the tree. I climbed up to the large branch and moved along it.

"What can you see, Peter?" Tara asked impatiently.

"Nothing," I said. "There's a tree in the way."

Holding carefully onto the branch, I crawled onto the wall and edged my way along it. Suddenly a loose piece of stone broke away and I slipped off the wall. I held tightly onto the branch as my legs dangled uselessly in the air.

"Peter, are you all right?" Tara called out anxiously as I tried desperately to swing myself back onto the wall.

Sparky barked madly from below and scratched at the tree. I finally managed to heave myself back onto the wall. I sat there for a moment, waiting to get my breath back.

"I'm OK," I replied.

"Can you see anything now?" Tara asked.

"Yes," I replied, "a house."

I was looking into the back garden of a small stone cottage. There was a path from the back door leading through a vegetable patch down to a large lawn. I moved along the wall to get a better view.

"Tara!" I cried. "There's been an accident! There's a man lying on the ground. He looks hurt – he's not moving!"

The man was covered in purple stains and was lying in the centre of the broken remains of what appeared to be a shed. A smashed timber panel lay to his side and broken glass was strewn over the lawn.

"I'm going over," I said. "See you at the gate."

I jumped down and dashed over to the gate. I tried to force the bolts open but they were too rusty and would not move. I looked around desperately for something to hit them with and finally found a large stone. I hammered the bolts hard and after a few attempts they slid back. I pulled the gate towards me. It opened a few centimetres, then jammed against the ground.

"Tara, push from your side," I yelled through the opening.

Tara pushed and I pulled as hard as I could. The gate

opened a little further and then stuck completely.

"It won't go any more, Peter!" she cried in frustration.

We tried again. Tara threw her weight against the door. Sparky joined in too – he barked and pawed at the gate. There was a creaking sound and a wooden slat broke away from the door panel. Sparky jumped through the small gap.

"Well done, Sparky," I said, patting him on the head. "Can you get through the gap, Tara?"

"Not quite," she replied.

We broke away more of the wooden slats and Tara squeezed through.

"Stay here, Sparky," I said, taking his lead out of my pocket.

"Woof," he barked indignantly.

"Sorry, Sparky, it's too dangerous," I said. "There's broken glass everywhere. I don't want you to get hurt."

I put Sparky on his lead and tied it to the gatepost. Tara and I ran over to the man and bent down to look at him. He had a deep cut in his forehead and blood had run down into his beard and onto the grass. His clothes were covered in purple stains.

"He looks terrible," Tara said, a worried look on her face. "We've got to get help. I'll go inside the house and phone for an ambulance."

As she got up the man groaned. He opened his eyes and raised a hand to his head.

"Are you OK?" I asked, concerned.

"My head hurts," he said quietly, "but I think I'm still alive."

"What happened?"

"Explosion," he replied.

"What…?" I began.

"Experiment," he said, attempting to sit up.

He lost his balance and swayed backwards. I reached out and grabbed one of his arms to steady him. Tara held onto the other

"Thank you," he said as we helped him to stand up.

He was a tall man with thick dark hair and grey streaks in his straggly beard. He was wearing pyjamas and a long green dressing gown.

"Let's get you into the house," Tara said softly.

We helped him along the cobbled path towards the back door of the house. As we reached it I could hear scratching and barking from inside. When I opened the door an enormous dog bounded out, nearly knocking us all over.

"Down, Sleepy, down girl," the man said to the dog.

"Sleepy!" I exclaimed. "She doesn't look very sleepy to me!"

Sleepy was the biggest, wildest and most active dog I had ever seen. She kept shaking the hair out of her eyes and wagging her huge tail. She jumped up at the man again, obviously delighted and relieved to see he was all right.

We went through the back door into the kitchen. I pulled out a chair from under the table and the man sat down.

"Can I get you anything?" Tara asked.

"A glass of water, please," he replied softly.

As Tara fetched the water I looked around the cluttered kitchen in amazement. I had never seen such a mess! Every surface was piled high with unusual looking things. There were crystals, fossils, rocks, bottles full of coloured liquids, an old radio lying on the draining board and a computer balanced delicately on the fridge.

Tara gave him the water and sat down.

"Thanks," he said, sipping it slowly.

He put the glass down on the table and smiled at us. His deep blue eyes were full of warmth and gentleness.

"Thank you for coming to help me," he said kindly. "My name is Professor P."

"I'm Peter."

"And I'm, Tara."

"How are you feeling, Professor P?" I asked.

"My head still hurts," he replied, "but I'll be OK."

"You really should go to the hospital and get it checked," she said seriously.

He hesitated and then nodded reluctantly. "Yes, I suppose you're right."

"Do you have a phone?" she asked. "We'd better call for an ambulance."

"A phone? Yes, there's one in here somewhere. Phone! Phone! Where are you?" he called out.

I looked at Tara. Why was Professor P calling for his phone? Perhaps the accident had affected his mind. He did seem rather confused.

"I'll get the phone for you, shall I, Professor P?" I asked.

"Thank you, but it's all right, Peter. I'll find it," he replied, looking around the room.

"Where are you phone?" he repeated sternly.

A little voice squeaked, "Here I am, Professor P, how may I be of assistance?"

Tara gasped. We looked at each other in astonishment. I could not believe what I had just heard – the phone had actually answered back!

"Sounds as if it's in the dog basket again," Professor P said, looking suspiciously at Sleepy.

Professor P stood up, wobbled and then sat down.

"Peter," he said, "would you mind getting it, please?"

I went over to the dog basket and found the phone under a blanket next to a large plastic bone. I picked it up and looked at it closely. It certainly looked like an ordinary phone. I wiped away the dog hairs and gave it to Professor P.

"Thank you," he said kindly. "Phone, call the hospital, please."

"Yes, Professor P. Right away," it chirped brightly.

Tara and I sat quietly as Professor P spoke to the hospital.

"They're sending an ambulance," he said as he put the phone down. "It should be here soon."

Sleepy quickly picked up the phone in her mouth and returned it to her basket.

"Very fond of that phone, she is," Professor P commented, looking rather puzzled.

He dabbed the cut on his head with a handkerchief and winced in pain.

"I need to get dressed," he said, standing up and walking shakily to the door. "Please help yourselves to something to drink, there's juice in the fridge. Oh, and there's a packet of chocolate chip cookies in the cupboard."

When he had left I looked around the kitchen in amazement. "Can you believe this place, Tara?" I said.

"I know!" she exclaimed. "I got such a shock when the phone spoke!"

I stood up and went over to the fridge.

"What would you like to drink, Tara?" I asked, reaching

out to open the fridge door.

"Orange juice, please," she replied.

"That's odd," I said, staring at the fridge. "There's no handle."

I tried to prise the door open but it would not budge. Tara came over and we pulled at it together.

"Would you mind not doing that?" said a deep, rather sombre voice.

We jumped back in surprise.

"Who said that?" I asked, turning round.

"I did," the fridge replied indignantly. "I asked you not to pull at me like that."

"Oh, er...sorry," I apologised.

"Now," it continued, "what do you want?"

Tara giggled. "Is it going to grant us three wishes?" she whispered.

"I do not do wishes," the fridge said dryly. "Just food and drink."

"Well, er... Could we have some orange juice then?" I asked.

"It wouldn't hurt to say please," the fridge said gruffly.

"Sorry," I said again.

"It's at the back on the left," the fridge said abruptly as the door sprang open.

I found the juice hidden behind some half-opened cans of cat food. Tara passed me two glasses and after pouring out the juice I put the carton back in the fridge. The door shut with a sigh.

"Doesn't harm to say thank you," it said sarcastically.

"Er, thank you very much," I said, embarrassed.

As I drank the juice I walked round the kitchen looking at everything with great interest. On one of the shelves was a bright orange toaster in the shape of a loaf of bread.

"I like this toaster," I said to Tara, chuckling.

"Toast? Did someone say toast?" it suddenly blurted out

in a bright and cheerful voice. "Would you like a piece?"

"Er…" I began.

"I make excellent toast," it interrupted. "Never burnt or underdone."

"No, no thanks," I stammered.

"Are you sure?" it pleaded.

"Yes," I replied.

"Yes, you want toast!" it cried in delight.

"No!" I said, confused. "I mean, yes, I'm sure I don't want toast."

"Oh," it squeaked disappointedly. "What a pity!"

"Maybe later," I added, feeling rather sorry for it.

"Oh, good, later will be fine," it chirped.

"What about a joke while we're waiting?" the toaster suggested. Before I could reply it continued, "Why were dinosaurs so wrinkled?"

"Sorry?" I said. Tara giggled at the surprised expression on my face.

"Because they never invented the iron!"

Without pausing it launched into the next joke, "How do you know when a dinosaur's been in the fridge?"

"I… I…" I began but, before I could answer, it squealed in delight. "There are footprints in the butter! Ha, ha, ha!"

Tara was now in stitches and had tears running down her cheeks.

"I see you found the toaster, Peter," said a voice from behind me. I spun round.

"Professor P, the toaster," I spluttered, "and the fridge!"

"Yes," he said as he went over to the toaster. "They both talk, but unfortunately this one doesn't know when to stop!"

"No, Professor P! Don't switch meeee…" the toaster fell silent as he pulled out the plug.

"Do all your inventions talk?" I asked, intrigued.

"Yes, most of them do," he said, sitting down at the

table. "Actually, you can have quite a sensible conversation with the fridge, although it can be a bit depressing sometimes."

"How do they work?"

"I see you have a curious mind, Peter," he replied, smiling. "It's quite simple really. Computer chips. They're all networked to a central computer in the basement..."

He was interrupted by a loud commanding voice. "Someone at the door, Sir!" it boomed.

I looked around to find out where the voice had come from.

"It's just the front door, Peter," Professor P laughed, seeing my surprise. "The ambulance must have arrived."

He stood up and got his coat from the hallway.

"Thank you so much for helping me," he said as he put on his coat. "Do come again when I'm feeling better, I'll show you some more of my inventions."

"Thanks," we said, "we'd love to."

We all went outside and the driver helped Professor P into the back of the ambulance.

"See you again soon," he called as the doors slammed shut.

The ambulance drove off. As I watched it disappear down the hill I was overcome with a tremendous feeling of excitement and adventure.

CHAPTER THREE

Inventions

Next morning Sparky and I dashed round to see Tara. We didn't have far to go – she only lived next door!

"Hi, Peter, hi, Sparky," she greeted us happily.

"Shall we go and see if Professor P is OK?" I asked.

Tara agreed. We walked along the estate and when we reached the main road Sparky and I turned left to go down the hill towards the sea.

"It's quicker to go this way," she said, pointing up the hill. "Here, I drew a sketch of the village from my OS map when I got home yesterday. Have a look."

Tara took a neatly folded piece of paper out of her pocket and gave it me.

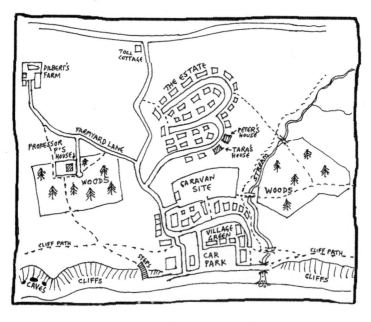

"I didn't realise you were an artist, Tara!" I said admiringly. She smiled.

Sparky was straining on his lead trying to pull me down the hill towards the sea.

"Come on, Sparky, we're going this way," I said, gently tugging on his lead.

We set off up the hill. When we reached the footpath through woods I let Sparky off his lead. He scampered away wagging his tail excitedly, obviously delighted to have found another new place to explore.

Ten minutes later we arrived at Professor P's house. I called to Sparky and opened the front gate. We walked down the moss-covered path to the front door of the cottage. It was an old stone building overgrown with ivy and red climbing roses. Sparky ran ahead and pawed expectantly at the front door. I looked for a doorbell but couldn't find one. I was about to knock when the door spoke.

"Welcome to Professor P's residence," it said in its deep booming voice. "Whom shall I say is calling?"

We all jumped back in surprise, startled by the loud authoritative voice.

"I'd forgotten Professor P's door spoke," I said to Tara.

"Me too," she laughed.

The door cleared its throat loudly. "Whom shall I say is calling?"

"Tara and Peter," Tara said.

"Oh, and Sparky too," I added.

"Please come in," the door said, opening in a slow and stately manner.

We went into the hall. Sleepy bounded down the stairs and greeted us enthusiastically. Professor P followed her, walking down slowly and carefully, holding tightly onto the banister. He had a large bandage on his head.

"Hello, Peter, hello, Tara," he said warmly. "How nice

to see you both again!"

"Are you feeling all right now, Professor P?" Tara asked.

"Not too bad, thank you," he replied with a smile. "The doctor convinced me nothing is broken." He touched the bandage gingerly and winced, "But I think I'd better be more careful next time I'm working on..." he stopped abruptly. "But never mind that now. How are you both? Would you like some tea?"

"Yes, please," we answered and followed him into the kitchen. As we sat down at the table, a fat fluffy tortoiseshell cat came through the cat-flap and rubbed its head against my legs.

"Oh, what a lovely cat!" Tara said, bending down to stroke it. "It's so soft."

"That's Cuddles," Professor P said. "Friendly little thing, isn't she? She's so sweet, wouldn't hurt a mouse."

Cuddles jumped up onto Tara's lap, settled down and began purring loudly.

"It was kind of you to help me yesterday," Professor P said as he brought the tea and a large plate of biscuits over to the table.

The cat-flap banged shut again. A small black cat jumped up onto the table and sniffed at the biscuits.

"What's this one called?" I asked, reaching out to stroke it.

"Careful, Peter!" Professor P warned.

I pulled my hand back, alarmed by his tone.

"That's Claws," he continued. "I wouldn't try to stroke him. Not unless you want to lose your fingers!"

Claws rolled onto his back and purred softly.

"Oh, I'm sorry, Claws," Professor P said, stroking the cat's tummy. "You can be very affectionate when you want to be. But you're not meant to be on the table."

Professor P pushed the cat gently and he jumped off the

table and leaped up onto the fridge.

"Have you always been an inventor, Professor P?" I asked, dunking a chocolate biscuit in my tea.

"Yes," he replied, "I've been inventing things in my spare time ever since I was a young boy but a few months ago I moved here and began to work on my inventions full-time."

"I'd like to be an inventor," I said. "I'm always thinking of ideas and making things."

"Yes, that's how I was when I was your age," Professor P chuckled. "Got me into quite a lot of trouble though. Never forget the time when the TV blew up after I'd made a few er… improvements to it."

Tara glanced at me and we laughed.

"What are you working on now, Professor P?" she asked.

"Oh, all sort of things!" he replied enthusiastically. "I'm really interested in ways to reduce pollution and save energy. But a lot of my inventions are just for fun, like the joke telling toaster you met yesterday!"

"Here is something I think you'll like," he said, reaching into his pocket. He took out a silver sphere the size of a cricket ball.

"What is it?" I asked curiously.

"This is Superbrain 3.01," he said proudly. "It's a computer, but not your average, ordinary computer. This one learns and thinks like we do."

I looked at him in surprise and then at the little silver sphere.

"A computer?" I said, staring at it. Surely Professor P was joking – it was far too small to be a computer. "But how? There's no screen, or keyboard or mouse…"

"Oh, no need for all that out-of-date stuff," he replied, chuckling, "or those infernal wires! No, Peter, this is a quantum computer!"

Professor P raised his hand, and like a magician performing a trick, he tapped the sphere twice.

Tara and I looked in astonishment as a large blue fluffy rabbit with a pink nose and long floppy ears popped into the air above the sphere.

"How…?" I began as the blue rabbit hovered above the table and began to chew on the end of one of its ears.

"Oh, it's really cute!" Tara cried.

"Superbrain is a highly intelligent and complex computer generated hologram. He can appear in any form he wants, but for some reason that I don't quite understand," Professor P said, scratching his head, "he often appears as a rabbit. Superbrain, I'd like you to meet my new friends Peter and Tara."

"Hello," the rabbit said shyly.

"Hello, Superbrain," I said curiously.

"You can call me Floppy," he said with a friendly smile.

I looked closely at Floppy. He was more like a cartoon rabbit than a real one. I noticed he was slightly fuzzy around the edges and in places I could almost see right through him.

"Woof!" Sparky barked, tilting his head suspiciously towards the rabbit.

Floppy jumped off the table onto the floor. He attempted to transform himself into a puppy and began by growing a long tail and then, rather unconvincingly, trying to wag it. After a few moments the change was complete and apart from the blue colour and the long ears, Floppy looked like a small Labrador puppy. Sparky looked at me warily with his big brown eyes and then at the strange creature in front of him. What was it? It looked like a puppy but it certainly didn't smell like one.

"Say hello to Floppy," I said encouragingly.

He put out his paw to touch Floppy but it passed right through the creature. Sparky yelped in surprise and ran over to me.

"It's OK, Sparky," I laughed stroking him reassuringly.

Floppy wagged his tail and approached Sparky who cautiously came out from behind my legs and sniffed at Floppy. Floppy sniffed back and then copied everything that Sparky did! Poor Sparky was so confused at first, but he finally decided that this 'dog' was friendly.

"Floppy's great!" Tara said as we watched the two puppies run around the room together.

"He's amazing," I agreed.

"Thank you," Professor P said proudly.

"How does he work?" I asked.

"Well, he's not like other computers," he explained. "They can only follow the programs they've been given. But Floppy can take his basic program and use it to learn from his experiences. In some ways he's almost like a young child, growing and learning all the time."

We watched Sparky playing happily with Floppy. Sparky was obviously delighted to have made a new friend!

"Would you like to see some of my other inventions?" Professor P asked.

"Yes, please!" we replied eagerly.

He stood up, paused and stroked his beard thoughtfully. "Now, what shall I show you first?" he mused.

He went over to a large cupboard under the sink, opened the door and took out an old battered cardboard box. Sleepy saw it and jumped up out of her basket. She barked furiously.

"Perhaps I'd better not show you these now," he said, replacing the box. "They're pet products," he whispered, "and Sleepy is still rather sensitive about them."

"Why's that?" Tara asked.

Professor P gave Sleepy a dog biscuit, patted her head and sat down at the table with us. He leaned forward and said in a hushed voice, "We had a slight accident recently with the automatic dog bathing machine. Did get her clean but I'm afraid she lost a few hairs in the process!"

"Woof, woof," Sleepy barked.

"Oh, yes, and there was that little incident with the electric flea comb," he continued.

Sleepy whimpered pathetically.

"I am sorry, Sleepy, will you ever forgive me?" Professor P continued in a softer voice as he stroked the dog's head.

"But the automatic pet feeder does work very well," he continued. "I always use it when I go away for a few days. It automatically opens the cans and puts out just the right amount of food and water."

Sleepy finished her dog biscuit and went over to the back door. Professor P opened the door and let her out. Sparky ran after her.

"Professor P, Professor P," a tiny voice squeaked as Professor P sat back down at the table.

He raised his left arm and I could see a purple watch on his wrist.

"What is it, Watch?" he asked.

"Professor P, it's time for lunch."

"Thank you, Watch," he said, "but it's only eleven thirty, I'll have lunch later."

"But, Professor P, you have an appointment with the bank manager at twelve thirty."

"Oh, yes, of course," he said, frowning.

"Shall we go now, Professor P?" I asked.

"No, no," he replied, "you're both most welcome to stay for lunch. I'll see what I can find to eat."

He went over to the cupboard by the fridge and opened the door. Two cans rolled out onto the floor.

"How about beans on toast?" he said as he picked them up.

"I'll have a carrot, please, Professor P," Floppy said, suddenly appearing as a rabbit again.

"Floppy," Professor P explained patiently, "you don't eat real carrots. You're not a real rabbit."

"Oops, I forgot," Floppy said, scratching his head. "But I'm hungry."

"Perhaps you could conjure up a holographic carrot then," Professor P suggested.

"Good idea!" Floppy said happily and a huge orange carrot appeared in his paw. He sank his teeth into it. "Delicious!" he cried as he munched on it noisily.

Claws suddenly jumped from the top of the fridge and landed on the table. He skidded across its surface and then pounced on Floppy. Floppy disappeared in a flash of blue light. The cat looked bewildered, lost its balance and fell off the table, landing on Professor P's lap.

"Over here, little pussy cat," Floppy called out as he reappeared on the other side of the room as a small white mouse with a long pink tail.

Claws jumped to his feet and glared at Floppy. He lowered his head and slowly waved his tail. He was getting ready to pounce again.

"Floppy!" Professor P said, raising his voice.

"Here pussy, pussy, I'm over here," laughed Floppy as he vanished again and reappeared back on the table.

"Stop that, Floppy!" Professor P cried.

Claws approached Floppy cautiously, inching towards him slowly. Suddenly Floppy transformed into a huge green dragon, turned towards Claws and blew bright orange flames out of his mouth. Claws jumped off the table and ran towards the cat-flap with Floppy in close pursuit. Claws wailed loudly and shot through the cat flap.

"Now look what you've done to that poor cat!" Professor P scolded Floppy.

"Sorry, I won't do it again," Floppy said, obviously not

in the least bit sorry. He shrank in size and became a rabbit again but still with a scaly green tail.

Professor P laid the table and put two slices of bread in the toaster. The toaster burst into life.

"Oh, thank you, thank you, thank you," it cried. "I will deliver the very best toast you have ever eaten in your whole life. And while you wait, may I entertain you with a few of my jokes?"

"No, thank you, Toaster," Professor P said politely. "Perhaps another time."

"Of course, Professor P," it chirped brightly.

"And now for the beans," he said, putting the two cans on the table. "No need for a saucepan with these."

I picked up one of the cans and examined it. It looked like an ordinary can but with a red button on the top that said *Press here firmly*.

"What does this do?" I asked, pointing to the button.

"It's a self-heating can," he replied, "my latest product. You press the red button, wait a few seconds and the beans are cooked. It's reusable and ideal for camping. I thought of the idea when I was out backpacking last summer and my stove ran out of gas."

"That's a really good idea," I said, picking up one of the cans. "Shall I press the button?"

"Nooooo…" Floppy cried, pretending to be horrified. He pulled his ears over his eyes and then disappeared.

"I think you'd better let me do it," Professor P said as he took the can from me. "I've, er… had a few problem ones. I think it will be safer if I do it over by the sink."

He put the can on the draining board, covered it with a cloth, pressed the red button and moved away quickly. A few seconds later there was a loud ping and Professor P went over to examine the can.

"Perfect," he said, obviously relieved. He grinned broadly as he pulled off the top of the can.

"Now for the toast," he said, walking over to the toaster.

I noticed a strong smell of burning. Two pieces of blackened toast popped up from the toaster.

"Sorry, Professor P," the toaster apologised. "I lost concentration, with all the excitement and everything."

"Hmm!" Professor P said, slightly annoyed. "Please be more careful this time!" He put two more slices of bread into the toaster and threw the others into the bin.

"Of course, Professor P," the toaster replied meekly.

He put the other can of beans on the draining board, pressed the button and moved away again. We waited expectantly.

Nothing happened.

"Looks like it's a dud," he said, looking cautiously at the tin. He went over to the can and was just about to pick it up when there was a loud bang and the top of the tin blew off.

Beans erupted out of the can and went everywhere. They covered Professor P's arm, the draining board and dripped onto the floor.

"Slightly too much pressure," he said calmly, wiping the beans from his jacket. "I need to iron out that bug."

Floppy appeared as a pink hyena and laughed loudly.

"Even the bugs have bugs!" he quipped.

"Never mind, Professor P," Tara said, "there's enough in this can for all of us."

I helped Professor P clear up the mess while Tara buttered the perfectly done toast and shared out the beans. We chatted happily over lunch and watched Floppy entertain us with his various antics. Afterwards we cleared away the plates and Professor P put them in the dishwasher.

"Short wash, please, low temperature," he said to the dishwasher as he shut the door.

Nothing happened.

"Oh, silly me!" he laughed as he switched it on. "It's just an ordinary dishwasher – I haven't made any improvements to it yet. But, I've got great plans," he added with a knowing smile.

Professor P's watch chirped up again, "Don't forget the time, Professor P!"

"Oh, yes," he sighed, "I must keep that appointment."

I called Sparky in from the garden.

"It was nice to see you both again," Professor P said as we stepped out of the front door.

"Thanks for showing us your inventions," I said enthusiastically.

"And for lunch," Tara added.

"You're welcome," Professor P said, beaming. "Please come again, any time, just drop round, or give me a call." He put his hand into the inside pocket of his jacket, "Here's my card."

He gave us both a small silver card. It had four holographic pyramids in the corners and bright green lettering that said:

CHAPTER FOUR

The Fossil Shop

We left Professor P's house and decided to go down to the beach. As we walked along the footpath over the hills we chatted excitedly about Professor P's inventions. We both thought Floppy was great fun!

When we reached the beach I squinted at the bright sun reflecting off the hot pebbles.

"It's a good day for a swim," Tara said, looking out to sea.

"Good idea!" I said, wiping the sweat off my brow.

"No waves though," she added. "We'll have to go surfing another time."

We decided to go home for our swimming things and walked along the beach to the car park. As we went up the road to our estate Tara suggested we go into the village and get an ice cream. I happily agreed!

We turned right off the main road into the village. I had not been there before and looked around curiously at the pretty village square. It had an old church, a pub and some shops neatly arranged around a large square green. I could see a baker's, a newsagent's, a small post office, a general store and a gift shop that had post cards and beach things outside.

"That's a new shop over there!" Tara said as we crossed the green. "I wonder what it sells."

We ran over to have a closer look. A man was on a ladder painting a sign. It said *The Foss* in large gold letters. The windows were covered in newspapers so we could not see inside.

The door was ajar and Sparky ran into the shop.

"Mind your dog!" the man called out, "the paint's still

wet!"

"Sparky! Come here!" I shouted after him. We waited for him but he did not come out.

"Oh, we'd better go and get him," I said finally. We opened the door and went into the shop.

Large cardboard boxes were piled all over the floor. A woman looked up from her unpacking and smiled.

"I'm afraid we're not open yet," she said politely.

The woman had deep brown eyes and curly brown hair that flowed down to her shoulders. She was wearing a long lavender coloured dress covered with silver stars and she had a large purple crystal pendant around her neck.

"We're sorry to disturb you," I began, "but…"

At that moment Sparky ran over to her. He circled her playfully and flicked the tassels on the bottom of her dress with his paws.

"Oh, what a lovely puppy!" she said, stroking him gently.

"He ran in by himself," I explained, "he's very nosey."

"Don't worry, I know what these young dogs are like. I used to have a Labrador just like him when I was a girl. What's this young fellow called?"

"Sparky," I said, relieved she was not cross.

"Hello, Sparky, I'm Mary."

We introduced ourselves and Tara asked Mary what she was going to sell in her shop.

"This is a fossil shop," she replied.

"Brilliant!" Tara exclaimed.

"You're interested in fossils then?" Mary said, smiling.

"Oh, yes," Tara replied. "I really like collecting fossils. I've found lots of really good ammonites on the beach!"

"Sounds like you're an expert!" Mary laughed. "Would you like to see some of my fossils?"

"Yes, please," we replied.

Mary reached into one of the opened boxes, took out a

fossil and gave it to us. It was a little smaller than my hand and had a beautiful spiral pattern on the shell. It looked like one of the ammonites we had found on the beach but it was polished and shone a lovely milky white colour.

"It looks like an ammonite," I said, looking carefully at the fossil.

"That's right, Peter," Mary replied. "Did you know they used to be called snake-stones? People believed they had magical powers. They're still very popular fossils – in fact, I've got two very large boxes of them to unpack!"

"Would you like some help?" Tara asked eagerly.

"We could help you put them out on the shelves too, if you like," I added.

"Thank you," Mary replied. "Let's start with this box here."

She opened a large cardboard box and we began to take out and unwrap the fossils. Sparky joined in as usual. He wagged his tail happily as he put his nose into the box. He was more interested in playing with the wrapping paper than the fossils though!

"What are these, Mary?" Tara asked as she unpacked a collection of fossils that looked like the 'hedgehog spines' we had found on the beach.

"They're called belemnites," she replied. "They were small squids."

"Squids?" I said in surprise. "Not hedgehogs?"

Mary laughed. "The pointed part is the fossilised remains of the backbone. The rest of the animal rots away."

"What's this one, Mary?" I asked as I unwrapped something that looked like a giant woodlouse.

"It's called a trilobite," she explained, "That's only a small one – some were a metre long!"

"A metre!" we exclaimed, horrified.

Mary laughed at the expression on our faces!

"Oh, this is beautiful!" Tara exclaimed, picking up a

beautiful piece of clear yellow stone.

"It's amber," Mary said. "It comes from the sap of trees. When the resin hardens insects are sometimes trapped inside. If you look carefully…"

"Oh, yes!" Tara cried, holding it up to the light. "I can see a tiny mosquito!"

The next few hours flew by as we continued unpacking and discovering new and fascinating fossils. Mary suggested that we use the ones we had unpacked to make our own display in the large glass cabinet in the centre of the shop. We dusted the fossils, put price stickers on them and, with Mary's help, arranged them neatly in the cabinet.

"It's almost three o'clock," Mary said as we finished our display. "Time for a tea break, I think. Would you like some cakes from the baker's?"

"Yes, please," I said, suddenly feeling rather hungry.

"What about Sparky?" Mary asked.

"I've got some dog biscuits for him," I replied, "he'll be fine, thank you."

Mary left the shop and I gave Sparky his biscuits. He ate them eagerly and then curled up in the corner of the room and fell asleep. Mary returned a few minutes later with a selection of cakes. She went into a room at the back of the shop and made a pot of tea. When she returned we put a sheet of cardboard on the stone floor and all sat down.

"When will you be opening the shop, Mary?" Tara asked.

"The end of the week, hopefully," she replied. "I've been looking forward to this moment for many years."

"Is this your first shop?" I asked.

"Yes," Mary replied. "I've never run a shop before. I worked in an office after I finished my Geology degree. But this is what I've always wanted – to live by the sea and have my own fossil shop. And now my dream's come true!"

Mary's eyes lit up as she looked around the shop and told us all her plans for it.

We finished our cakes and spent the rest of the afternoon helping Mary. By five o'clock we had unpacked the last box. Mary went into the back room and returned with a large wooden display cabinet. Inside, I could see the fossilised remains of a large fish-like creature that had a long pointed mouth, rows of sharp teeth and large round eyes.

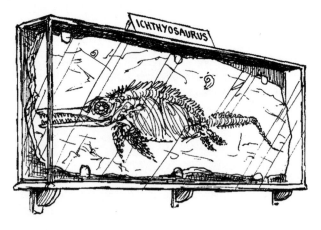

"What is it?" I asked curiously.

"An ichthyosaurus, a fish lizard." Mary replied.

"It's enormous!" Tara exclaimed.

"And this one's only a baby," Mary laughed. "You should see the adults! They could grow to be as large as a crocodile and just as powerful. They could crush an ammonite shell with one snap of those jaws."

As I gazed at the fossil it seemed to look back at me with its wide staring eyes. I wondered what it had been like when it was alive.

"They were quite common in the Jurassic Period," Mary explained. "Life was very different then – fierce dinosaurs ruled the land and huge reptiles roamed the seas. It certainly would have been an exciting time to live!"

We helped Mary fix the cabinet above a shelf on the wall, then stood back to admire it.

"Is it very valuable?" Tara asked as she gazed at the creature.

"Oh, yes," Mary replied. "If it was for sale I'd ask at least ten thousand pounds for it."

"Ten thousand pounds!" I cried in astonishment – I had no idea fossils could be so valuable.

"Yes, but I don't intend to sell it," Mary continued. "I wouldn't part with it for anything. I found it myself when I was thirteen years old. It took months of hard work to chisel away all the rock and clean the fossil. No," she said, "I wouldn't part with my 'baby' for anything."

"Do you think we could find one, Mary?" Tara asked excitedly.

"Well, it's possible," she replied. "You're certainly in the right place. The Jurassic Coast is one of the best places in the world to find fossils. But if you're going to become professional fossil hunters, you will need the right tools."

Mary went into the back room and returned a few moments later with a plastic box. She opened it and took out a hammer, a pair of glasses and a set of small chisels. Tara and I looked at them with interest.

"You need a special hammer and chisels like these to break the fossil-bearing rocks open," she said, "and these safety goggles to protect your eyes."

She reached into the box and took out a collection of smaller tools, including files, wire brushes and what looked like a set of sharp pointed dentist tools.

"When you've cleared most of the rock away from the fossil you need these to get into the gaps." She held up the pointed tools. "And then a wire brush to bring out the shine."

Mary put the tools neatly back into the box and closed the lid.

"Would you like to have these?" she asked, holding the box out to us, "as a gift. You've been so much help today, I'll be able to open the shop a day early."

"Oh, thank you!" we cried in delight.

"My pleasure," Mary said, smiling. "You'll find the best fossils in the rocks at the bottom of the cliffs. But don't climb the cliffs, they're too dangerous."

"We'll be careful," we promised.

I gently woke up Sparky and we went over to the door.

"Thanks for your help today," Mary said as we left the shop. "Come and see me again and show me what you've found."

"We will," we replied.

"Good luck," she called as she closed the door.

CHAPTER FIVE

Gold

The first few weeks of my new life on the Jurassic Coast were fantastic! Each morning I would wake to the sound of Sparky scratching at my bedroom door, ready to run down to the beach to play. I would draw back the curtains and the sun would stream into my new room. I would open my window, look out onto the rolling hills and hear the cries of seagulls and the sound of waves breaking in the distance.

Every day was a holiday – Tara, Sparky and I would go swimming or surfing in the sea, walking on the hills, exploring the woods or looking for fossils. One day we discovered a small fossil fish. We rushed over to the Fossil Shop to show Mary. She was very excited, as she had never seen one quite like it before. We carefully cleaned and polished the fossil and then searched through her reference books to find out what it was. It turned out to be a rare type of leptolepis, and quite valuable.

We had a brilliant time with Professor P, Sleepy and Floppy too! We went to visit them often and had great fun helping Professor P test his new 'outdoor range' of ecological inventions. One afternoon we all rushed down to the beach to try out his solar-powered filter kettle. We filled it with seawater, left it in the sun for an hour to boil and then made a cup of tea. It did taste rather salty at first but after Professor P made some adjustments to the kettle, it worked perfectly. We had great fun with his solar-powered self-inflating dinghy too and spent all afternoon in it, riding over the waves.

It seemed as though our holiday would last all summer. But on a hot afternoon in August something happened that would be the start of an amazing adventure and change our lives forever. Tara, Sparky and I were on the beach, looking for fossils.

"Tara, come over here!" I called out.

"What is it, Peter?"

"Come quick!" I shouted, eager to show her what I had found.

Tara rushed over. I had just cracked open a small brown stone. It had shattered into dozens of pieces.

"Look at this!" I said excitedly.

"It looks like…" she stopped and looked at me in astonishment.

She picked up one of the pieces. It sparkled brilliantly in the sunlight. She looked at the silvery yellow metallic crystals and then at me again.

"Gold?" she said.

I nodded excitedly. "It must be worth a fortune!" I said, looking at the golden crystals scattered on the ground.

We hurriedly knelt down and gathered up all the pieces of the golden ore.

"Come on, let's look for some more!"

We put the gold in our pockets and walked along the beach, scanning the ground for more of the brown stones. Sparky joined in our search. He splashed madly into all the rock pools and scrabbled at the stones with his paws.

"I think I've found one!" Tara cried out.

I rushed over to her and examined the small brown stone. It looked like a small dried apricot, dark brown in colour, with strange dimples covering the surface. It was quite heavy.

"Yes," I nodded, "it's just like the one I found. Break it open, Tara!"

I watched as she hit the stone with a rock. It broke into three pieces. But there was no gold inside – it was just an ordinary stone.

"Never mind," Tara said, "let's keep looking!"

We continued to search the rock pools thoroughly and broke open many more promising stones but without finding any more gold. After an hour of searching in the hot afternoon sun we stopped to take a rest and have a drink.

"Peter," Tara said quietly, a serious expression on her face. "Do you think we should tell anyone about the gold, or shall we keep it a secret?"

"Let's keep it a secret for now," I replied. "At least until we've found some more."

"OK," she nodded. "Come on, let's keep looking."

We spent the rest of the afternoon trying to find more of the gold-bearing stones but without success.

"I wish we could find some more," I sighed wearily. "There are just so many pebbles to sort through. It's like trying to find a needle in a haystack."

"Maybe we could train Sparky to sniff it out!" Tara suggested. I laughed.

"I know," she cried suddenly. "We could use a metal detector. I saw this great program on TV a few weeks ago – they were using one to find buried treasure. I'm sure it would work!"

"Of course," I said excitedly, "that's a brilliant idea! I wonder where we could get one from?"

Before Tara had time to reply Sparky jumped up and started wagging his tail. I looked up and noticed Professor P and Sleepy walking towards us from beyond the cliffs. Professor P was weighed down with a large rucksack and Sleepy was carrying two cloth bags, tied together and draped over her back like saddlebags. We waved and ran over to meet them.

"Hello, Peter, hello, Tara," Professor P greeted us with a friendly smile. "Such a lovely day, have you come out for a swim?"

"No," I replied. "We've been looking for..."

"Oh, out looking for fossils, were you?" he asked, finishing my sentence. "Found anything interesting?"

"Er, not yet," Tara answered awkwardly.

"Never mind," he said encouragingly. "I'm sure you'll find some soon. I found a lovely ammonite the other day."

As we chatted away about fossils it occurred to me that Professor P would probably know about metal detectors. I asked him if he knew how much they cost and where we could buy one.

"Buy one!" he exclaimed in horror. "You don't need to do that! You can easily make one. I'd be happy to show you how. If you like we can go back to my house and start straight away. I've got all the electronics you'll need."

Tara looked at me and nodded excitedly.

"Thanks!" we cried. "That would be brilliant."

We walked slowly back along the beach towards the steps in the cliff, stopping a few times for Professor P to adjust his rucksack. Tara, Sparky and I climbed the steps and waited for Professor P and Sleepy as they struggled up behind us. When he reached the top Professor P stopped to take off his rucksack and have a rest.

"What have you been doing on the beach today, Professor P?" Tara asked.

"Oh, er, I was…" he hesitated and then added with a mysteriously smile, "I was trying out a new invention."

Professor P gave Sleepy a drink of water and after a short rest we set off along the footpath over the hills. When we reached the woods Professor P and Sleepy went ahead along the narrow path through the trees. Tara and I hung back, waiting for Sparky.

"I wonder what Professor P's new invention is," I said curiously to Tara.

"Me too," she whispered. "He was very mysterious about it, wasn't he?"

Sparky ran over to us and we followed Professor P and

Sleepy into the woods.

"Finally home!" Professor P sighed as we arrived at his house. We went into the hallway and he carefully took off his rucksack. "Thank you, Sleepy," he said as he untied the bags from her back and stroked her affectionately.

"Woof," she barked and licked his hand before running off into the garden with Sparky.

"Now, let's see what we've got for this metal detector," Professor P said as we went into the kitchen. He began rummaging through the cupboards and quickly produced a collection of old radios, broken circuit boards and coils of wire.

"I made my first metal detector when I was only twelve years old," he said as he put a pile of electronics onto the table. "All you need is a large coil of wire, a simple electronic circuit and a pair of headphones."

He continued to search through the cupboards and the pile of components grew bigger.

"There, that should be enough," he said, putting a pair of headphones on the top of the pile. "Oh, I didn't ask, what do you want the metal detector for? Looking for anything in particular?"

"Oh, er…" I replied, feeling very awkward about not sharing our secret with Professor P. "We er…wanted one to…"

"Look for treasure!" Tara added quickly with a smile.

"Good idea," Professor P chuckled. "Let me know if you find any pirate's gold!"

"We will," I smiled.

"Good, well now, have you ever used a soldering iron before?" Professor P asked, rolling up his sleeves.

"No," we replied, staring at the mountain of old rubbish on the table.

"In that case," he said, "I'll give you a soldering iron each and you can practice using it to unsolder the components you'll need from these old circuit boards. When you've got the hang of it we can start making the metal detector circuit itself."

He brought over two soldering irons and plugged them into the mains socket in the wall by the table. When they had warmed up he showed us how to use them.

"Now, be careful!" he warned. "The ends of these soldering irons are very hot indeed. Make sure you put them back in their stands when you've finished with them."

Professor P watched carefully as we both unsoldered a few electronic components from the circuit board.

"Excellent," he said. "I'll leave you to practice. I need to take my equipment down to the basement and sort out a few things. I'll leave Floppy with you. He can show you what components to unsolder."

He took Floppy's sphere out of his pocket and put it on the table. A blue rabbit appeared and said politely, "Hello, Peter, hello, Tara. How are you today?"

"Fine thanks, Floppy," we said. "We're going to make a metal detector."

"Oh, goody," he said excitedly. "Can I help?"

"Yes, please, Floppy," Professor P replied. "Peter and Tara are going to unsolder some components from these old circuit boards. Can I leave you in charge while I go downstairs, please?"

"Of course, Professor P," Floppy answered proudly.

"I'll see you shortly then," he said, leaving the room.

As soon as Professor P had gone Floppy changed into a large grey owl with big round black spectacles perched on the end of his beak.

He spoke with a posh schoolmaster's voice, "So, we are going to make a metal detector today?"

"No, Floppy," I laughed. "We're just going to practice with the soldering irons until Professor P comes back."

"Oh, you don't need to do that," he said firmly. "With

my expert advice we can make the metal detector quite easily and quickly."

"Do you really know how to make one, Floppy?" Tara asked, a little unsure.

"Of course," he replied confidently.

"OK," we said, "what do we do?"

"First, you need to unsolder all these capastulators, resistulators and transfibulators," he said, pointing to the various electronic components. "And then just do exactly what I tell you."

We followed Floppy's instructions precisely. "Wire that large round black capastulators to the small square resistulators there... add another capastulator there... now wire in the battery compartment, and another...and another – we'll need plenty of power...connect up the on/off switch. Well done! It's finished. Now put in the batteries and switch it on."

"Are you sure about this, Floppy?" I asked, staring at the strange circuit we had made.

"You doubt me!" he replied indignantly.

I flicked the switch. There was a loud bang! One of the components blew up in a puff of smoke and the horrid smell of burning plastic filled the air.

Moments later Professor P burst into the room. "Is everyone all right?" he cried.

He looked around and saw the smoke rising from the monstrous collection of tangled wires and components that was our 'metal detector'. Floppy shrank in size and turned bright pink.

"Oh, Floppy!" Professor P cried. "What have you done?"

For once Floppy was at a loss for words.

"I hope we didn't harm anything, Professor P," Tara said anxiously.

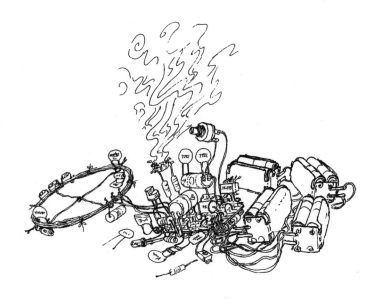

"Oh, no, it's all right," he replied, "these are just old components, I've got plenty more."

He examined the circuit on the table and chuckled. "What a mess! But at least you've learnt how to solder!"

"I think it needed more capastulators," Floppy said sheepishly.

"Capastulators!" Professor P exclaimed. "They're called capacitors, Floppy – and there's quite enough of them in the circuit already!"

"Sorry, Professor P," Floppy said quietly.

"Oh, it's not your fault, Floppy," he said kindly, "I think I need to have another look at your electronics program."

Professor P's watch suddenly piped up, "Professor P, Professor P!"

"Yes, Watch, what is it?"

"It's five thirty. You asked me to tell you when it was five thirty."

"Did I?" he asked, scratching his head. "Now why was that?"

"Sorry, I can't remember," the watch squeaked, "but you said it was important."

"I think we ought to be going home for tea now anyway, Professor P," I added. "Sorry about all the mess."

"No need to worry about that, Peter, we can sort it out tomorrow…"

"Ah, that's it!" he exclaimed, "I'm sorry, I'm busy tomorrow. Can you come Thursday instead, after lunch? I'll draw up a circuit diagram for the metal detector and we should be able to finish it then in a few hours."

"Thanks, Professor P," we said as we left the house. "We'll see you on Thursday."

CHAPTER SIX

The Basement

On Thursday afternoon Tara and I rushed over to Professor P's house eager to finish our metal detector. When we arrived the front door greeted us in its usual pompous manner.

"Professor P is not at home," it said.

"Oh," I said, taken aback. "He asked us to come today, after lunch."

"He did not inform *me* of that," the door said self-importantly.

"Maybe we're too early," Tara suggested, glancing at her watch. "It is only two o'clock. Let's come back later."

As we started to walk away the door boomed out after us. "Wait! Floppy wishes to talk to you. He says it is important. You'll find him in the kitchen."

The door swung open. Sparky bounded inside and Tara and I followed him into the hall. Sleepy ran down the stairs and greeted us enthusiastically. She wagged her tail wildly and was obviously delighted to see us.

"Hi, Sleepy," I said, stroking her head.

We went into the kitchen and found Floppy floating above the table. The little rabbit was covered in pink spots and had a thermometer in his mouth.

"Oh, Floppy, what's the matter?" Tara asked.

"I'm not feeling well," he whimpered.

"Oh, I'm sorry to hear that," she said kindly. "What's wrong with you?"

"I caught a virus," he said pathetically, "when I went on the Internet last night."

Tara looked at me doubtfully and whispered, "Is that possible?"

I shrugged.

"Or it might just be a bug," he sniffed. "If only Professor P was here, he could make me better," he said and blew his nose very loudly on a spotted handkerchief.

"Where is he?" I asked.

"I wish I knew. I'm ever so worried. I think something terrible has happened. He just disappeared."

"Disappeared?" Tara said in surprise. "When did you last see him?"

"Tuesday night," Floppy replied. "He was in the basement. He was really excited. He said he was going to do something important. And he asked me to do two things."

"What were they, Floppy?" I asked.

"The first thing was..." he scratched his head and paused.

"I don't remember," he said finally in a quiet sad voice.

"And the second thing?" Tara asked.

"Er, no, I don't remember that either. My head hurts, Tara."

"I'm really sorry, Floppy," she said gently. "Can't you remember anything at all?"

"No," he sniffed, "the last thing he said to me was to stop pretending to be ill. He said I couldn't possibly have caught a computer virus from playing on the Internet and to pull myself together."

"Oh, poor, Floppy," Tara giggled and smiled at me.

"I'm worried that Professor P has had an accident," Floppy said. "Like last time, when the shed blew up."

"Let's check outside," I suggested.

We went into the garden and over to the shed. It had been roughly patched together. Sparky scratched at the door. I tried the handle but it was locked.

"It's empty," Tara said, peering in through the window.

"He might be in the basement," Floppy said. "That's where he does most of his experiments. Let's go down there."

"Well," I said doubtfully. "I don't really think we should go snooping around."

"You must!" Floppy cried anxiously. "Professor P has been missing since Tuesday. Who knows what might have happened to him! He might be lying injured in the basement!"

"We'd better check," Tara said anxiously.

Floppy led us through the hallway to a door under the stairs. We went into what appeared to be a small broom cupboard. I switched on the light. At the end of the cupboard I saw a narrow flight of stairs leading down into the darkness. Tara went down first and Sparky started after her.

"No, Sparky," I said, pulling him back. "You stay here with Sleepy."

He barked indignantly. I stroked his head and gently guided him back into the hall with Sleepy. I shut the cupboard door and slowly climbed down the rickety old wooden stairs. After a few metres the wooden stairs joined a much stronger metal spiral staircase that led down into the darkness below.

"I can't see a thing," Tara said when we reached the bottom.

"Professor P," she called out. "Are you there?"

There was no reply.

I fumbled around, trying to find a light switch.

"There's got to be one somewhere," I said. "Do you know where the light switch is, Floppy?"

"There's no switch," he replied. "You have to talk to the lights."

"I should have guessed," I said, laughing and then called out. "Lights!"

Nothing happened.

"I think you have to say please," Floppy added.

"Lights, please," I shouted, feeling rather silly.

"No need to shout," came the reply, as the basement was flooded with light.

I gasped in surprise. The basement was gigantic – bigger than the whole cottage above. It was a dome shaped cavern with corridors leading out in all directions like spokes from a wheel. The floor looked like a rubbish tip – it was littered with bits of old cars, broken televisions, vacuum cleaners, computers and even an old telephone box! The mountain of junk was piled so high that, in places, it almost reached the ceiling.

"How ever did he get all this in here?" Tara cried in

astonishment.

Floppy called out loudly to Professor P.

"Oh, no, he can't hear us!" Floppy cried. "I knew it! He's probably lying unconscious somewhere. We'd better check all the rooms!"

Floppy rushed off into the nearest corridor and waited for us. "Hurry up!" he called out impatiently.

"This place is amazing!" I said to Tara as we carefully weaved our way through the piles of junk. "I wonder what on earth Professor P's been working on down here."

"I can't imagine!" she said, staring at an old fridge, lying on its side with its insides exposed.

Floppy was waiting for us outside a blue door with a sign on it saying *Useful Utilities*. I opened the door and looked inside. The room was large and square. On the workbench opposite the door was a large green box surrounded by wires and pieces of metal and plastic.

"I wonder what this is," I said, going over to the box. It had a blue honeycombed panel on the lid. I lifted the lid and we peered inside. It was full of wires and tubes coiled into some very strange shapes.

"Weird," Tara said. "Do you know what it does, Floppy?"

"It's a solar-powered cool box," he replied. "Professor P made it from an old fridge. I think he was having a few problems with it though."

"There's not much room for the food," I commented.

"That's one of the problems," Floppy said sadly. "Come on! We must keep looking for Professor P."

As we worked our way away along the corridor, checking all the rooms, I was filled with a mounting sense of excitement. I never realised Professor P had a secret Aladdin's Cave, full of amazing inventions! One room, called *Ridiculous Robots,* was filled with brightly coloured robot parts and had a half-assembled robot lying by the door. The room at the end of this corridor was called *Terrible Toys* and Tara and I rushed inside, wondering excitedly what we would find.

"Oh," I said disappointedly. "Not much in here."

The room was empty except for an opened cardboard box resting on the workbench. I went over to it and looked inside. It was full of small brightly coloured plastic balls. I picked one up and saw a tiny battery and circuit inside.

"What do you think they do?" I said, showing it to Tara.

"Maybe you should drop it and find out," she said playfully.

As I dropped the ball Floppy cried out, "No, Peter!"

But it was too later. The ball hit the floor and bounced back at me with such speed that it almost hit me in the face! It bounced again, getting higher and higher!

"Quick! Catch it before it hits the ceiling!" Floppy said.

I tried to catch the ball but missed. It hit the ceiling, rebounded at enormous speed and passed right through Floppy.

"Look out, Tara!" I cried as it hit the wall and bounced straight at her.

She ducked just in time. The ball flew around the room, bouncing off the walls at terrifying speed. I tried again to catch it but missed and knocked over the whole box of balls. Dozens of the plastic balls tumbled onto the floor and burst into life. Suddenly the whole room was filled with bouncing balls, flying in every direction at ever increasing speed.

"Ow!" I cried as one hit me on the back of the head.

"Run for it, Peter!" Tara cried, shielding her face with her hands and racing for the door.

We dived into the corridor and slammed the door shut behind us. We waited outside for a few moments to catch our breaths and listened to the sound of the balls hammering against the door.

"Now I know why they're called *Terrible Toys*," I panted.

"I hope we didn't do any harm," Tara added.

"Don't worry," Floppy said. "That happened to Professor P last time he was in there. That's why he cleared all his tools out of the room. But come on," he urged, "we must keep looking."

We went back to the main storage area and continued searching along the next corridor. We looked in *Complex Computers*, *Seriously Silly* and *Fun Foods* but found no sign of Professor P. An hour later, as we worked our way along the last corridor, Floppy became more and more worried about Professor P.

"He must be in the basement! He must be," Floppy kept repeating to himself.

"Well, I think we've come to the last room," I said as we reached a door labelled *Impossible Ideas*.

I opened the door and we went inside. Unlike the other rooms it was spotless and uncluttered. Opposite the door was a desk with a new computer on it.

"The computer's still on!" I said in surprise.

On the screen was a drawing of a pyramid rotating slowly and beneath it were lines of mathematical equations.

"Do you know what it is, Floppy?" I asked.

"It's a… um, er…" he hesitated and then said quietly, "no, I'm sorry, I can't remember."

"Never mind," Tara said kindly.

Above the computer was a shelf stacked with long tubes.

"I wonder what these are," I said, picking one up. The tube was hollow and made of clear plastic. I picked up another one that was filled with bright yellow liquid. It felt slightly sticky so I carefully put it back.

"Well, we've looked everywhere now," Tara said as we left the room. "And there's no sign of Professor P."

"Oh, where is he?" Floppy cried, now quite distraught.

"Don't worry," Tara reassured him. "I'm sure he'll be back soon."

As we walked back along the corridor and up the stairs I felt very relieved we had found no sign of an accident. We left the basement and went back up to the kitchen. Sparky and Sleepy bounded over to us. The cats meowed loudly and rubbed up against our legs.

"She's hungry," Tara said, bending down to stroke Cuddles. "Do you think we should feed the cats?"

"OK," I said. "Let's give them their tea now, in case Professor P gets back late. We can leave him a note to say we fed them."

Sleepy ran up to the cupboard and put her paw on the handle.

"Oh, you're hungry too, are you, Sleepy?" I laughed.

I opened the cupboard door and took out the cans of pet food. Tara found a memo board on the fridge and wrote a quick note to Professor P.

"Tara, ask if we can come tomorrow morning to finish the metal detector," I said as I gave Sleepy her food.

"Good idea," Tara replied.

I called to Sparky and we went to the front door.

"Let's say goodbye to Floppy before we leave," Tara said.

"Where is he?" I asked, suddenly realising we had not seen him since leaving the basement.

Floppy's sphere was still in my pocket. I took it out, put it on the hall table and tapped it twice. The little rabbit appeared, looking very miserable indeed.

"I switched myself off," he said quietly, "so I wouldn't worry so much. Is Professor P home yet?"

"No, not yet," I replied. "But I'm sure he'll be back soon. We're going home for tea now. We'll come round tomorrow."

"Don't go!" Floppy cried in alarm. "You can't leave while Professor P is still missing."

"Don't worry, Floppy," Tara added. "I'm sure he'll be home soon. We'll see you in the morning."

"OK," he sniffed and disappeared again.

We left the house and set off along Farmyard Lane.

"I've never seen anything like Professor P's basement!" I said as we walked down the road towards our estate.

"I know!" Tara cried. "So many inventions! How does he think of them all!"

"Those bouncing balls were pretty scary though," I said, rubbing the sore spot on the back of my neck. "I hope we didn't do any harm. I think I'd better ring Professor P tonight and say sorry about the mess we made and explain what we were doing in the basement."

"Good idea," Tara said as we stopped outside her house. "I hope Floppy will be OK. You don't think he's right, do you? About Professor P having an accident?"

"No," I replied. "I expect he's just been delayed somewhere. You know what Floppy's like – he's always getting things wrong!"

"True," she agreed. "I'll come round tomorrow after breakfast then. You can tell me what Professor P said and we can go and finish the metal detector."

"OK," I replied. "See you tomorrow, Tara."

I spent the evening playing on my computer and at nine o'clock I decided to ring Professor P.

"Good evening, Professor P Products," his answer machine said in a rather self-important tone.

"Can I speak to Professor P, please?" I asked.

"If you're selling double glazing or fitted kitchens…" it said curtly.

"I'm not. I was just…"

"Or mobile phones or holidays…"

"This is, Peter!" I said in frustration. "I'm a friend of

Professor P's. I'd like to know if he's back home yet."

"Oh, sorry," it apologised, "I'll see if I can find him. Please hold the line. Let me entertain you with a relaxing song while you wait."

A loud wailing noise screeched out from the phone. The sound was out of tune and far from relaxing. I held the phone away from my ear until it stopped.

"I am afraid Professor P is not at home," it said. "Can I take a message?"

"Oh," I said, rather surprised and taken aback. "Er...can you just tell him Peter called and ask him to ring me when he gets back, please."

"Certainly," the phone replied. "Goodbye, and thank you for calling."

I put the phone down.

"Professor P still not home!" I said, puzzled.

Where could he be?

CHAPTER SEVEN

The Safe

The following morning I woke late and felt very tired after a restless night. I was in the kitchen finishing my breakfast when Tara arrived.

"Hi, Peter," she said brightly as she sat down at the table with me. "Not still eating breakfast!" she laughed.

"I've only just got up," I said. "I couldn't sleep – I was worrying about Professor P."

"Why, has something happened?" she asked, suddenly concerned.

"I'm not sure," I replied. "I called him last night, about nine o'clock. He wasn't in, so I left a message on his answer phone, asking him to ring me when he got back."

"And has he called?"

"No," I said, "not yet."

"Well," she said thoughtfully, "perhaps he got back too late to return your call."

"I hope so," I said, "but if he's not home yet…"

"Let's go there right now and see if everything's all right," Tara interrupted.

"OK," I said, quickly finishing my cereal.

I called Sparky in from the garden and we raced over to Professor P's house. When we arrived we were greeted by Sleepy with a welcoming bark. As we went into the kitchen there was a chorus of voices from all Professor P's inventions.

"Have you seen Professor P?" the toaster piped. "It's past breakfast time and he hasn't had his toast yet."

"It really isn't good enough," the fridge said gruffly. "Leaving us all like this. I've got some very smelly cheese in here that needs clearing out."

Floppy appeared with large bags under his eyes. He looked very miserable and tired.

"Peter, Tara," he sniffed, "I'm so glad you're here. Professor P still isn't back. I've been up all night, trying to work out what's happened to him and I finally remembered something important."

"What?" we asked, waiting impatiently as he sniffed loudly and blew his nose on a large spotted handkerchief.

"Just before Professor P left he went into his study," Floppy replied. "He was in there for ages. I think he was probably writing up his diary. I'm sure if we go and look at what he wrote it will tell us where he is."

"I don't think we should do that, Floppy," Tara said. "We can't pry into Professor P's private things."

"But you have to!" Floppy cried. "Professor P disappeared on Tuesday evening and now it's Friday! He's never been away so long without telling me. You've got to help! Please," he begged.

Tara turned to me, "what do you think, Peter?" she asked.

"No," I said, "I don't think we should read Professor P's personal diary."

"It's not a *personal* diary!" Floppy said. "It's just where he writes up his experiments. He won't mind if you look at it. You only need to look at the last entry anyway – that will tell us where he is."

"Professor P has been gone a long time," Tara said thoughtfully. "And he did go away without leaving enough food for the animals. Perhaps Floppy's right, Peter."

I thought about what Floppy had said and how worried he seemed. Perhaps it would be all right if we just had a quick look at the last entry in Professor P's diary – it might give us a clue as to what had happened to him.

"All right, Floppy," I said. "Where is the diary?"

"In the study," he replied. "Follow me."

Floppy lead us out of the kitchen and into the living room. It was a comfortable looking room with a large open fireplace, an upright piano and books piled everywhere. We went over to a door opposite the fireplace. It had the words *Documents & Diaries* written on it in shiny gold letters.

I opened the door and we went into a small room. It was covered from floor to ceiling with shelves stacked high with dusty books and papers. I went over to one of the shelves, picked up one of the black books and blew the dust away.

"They're all really old," I said, blowing the dust away. "Do you know where his latest diary is, Floppy?"

"It's in the safe!" Floppy replied, pointing to a shiny metal box on a shelf by the window. We went over to the safe. On the front of the box was a keypad and above it, written in big red letters, the words *DANGER EXPLOSIVES!*

"Explosives!" I cried out in alarm.

"Yes," Floppy sniffed. "It explodes if you try to open it with the wrong combination."

"I don't like the sound of that!" Tara exclaimed. "Professor P doesn't want anyone to look in his safe!"

"Don't worry, Tara," Floppy said reassuringly. "It will be quite safe. Just press the red button on the keypad."

Tara looked at me doubtfully.

"Do you know the combination, Floppy?" I asked.

"No," Floppy admitted, "Professor P wouldn't tell me. He said I might forget it or get it wrong and then the safe would explode and all his work would be lost."

"Well, there's no way…" I began.

"It will be all right," Floppy interrupted. "We can just explain to the safe what has happened and ask it to open. Please press the button, Peter – it's the only way we'll find out what's happened to Professor P."

I hesitated and then slowly reached out my hand. I

pressed the button and quickly stepped away.

A stern voice boomed out of the safe, "You wish to open me."

"Y…yes," I stammered. "Can you open, please?"

"What is the combination?" the voice echoed.

"We don't know," Tara said nervously, "but perhaps you could just open anyway, if you don't mind."

"Well, I do mind," it boomed. "Enter the correct code or I will explode in five minutes."

"Don't do that!" I cried, staring in horror at the red light flashing above the explosives sign. "We're friends of Professor P."

"Please enter the combination on the keypad," it said coldly. "Explosion in four minutes and fifty seconds."

"Oh, Floppy!" I cried. "What do we do now?"

"I…er…don't know. Sorry," he said, covering his eyes with his long ears.

Tara rushed over to the safe. "Please help us," she said desperately. "It's really, really important. Professor P is missing, we think he put something inside you that will help us find him."

"Professor P missing?" the safe said in surprise.

"Yes," I replied. "He disappeared three days ago and nobody knows where he is. Floppy said the last thing he did on Tuesday evening was put his diary in you. We think it will tell us where he is."

"Oh, I see," the safe said softly. It paused briefly and then said, "I would like to help you but I'm afraid I can't. I can't possibly tell you the combination. I'm a safe. It's my job to keep things safe for Professor P. I have only one job to do and that's it. Some people might say it was boring, but it's my job and that's what I'm programmed to do. I really can't…"

"You must," Tara pleaded.

"No," it replied stubbornly. "Explosion in four minutes

twenty seconds."

"Safe, you've got to help!" Floppy cried in desperation. "Professor P is in grave danger!"

"Danger, danger you say!"

"Yes, and we have to help Peter and Tara find him."

"Professor P in danger," the safe repeated, flustered. "Well…" it paused, "if you're trying to help him, maybe I could…"

It paused again. "No, I just can't tell you the combination. But perhaps…"

"Yes," we said hopefully.

"I could just give you a clue," it said thoughtfully. "Yes, that's it, if I only give you a clue then I'm not actually telling you the combination and I'm still doing my job."

"Good idea!" I said encouragingly.

"OK, I'll do it," the safe finally agreed.

"Yes!" we cried in relief.

"There are three numbers," the safe explained. "Are you ready for the first clue?"

"Yes," I said anxiously.

"Chewed and swallowed."

"What?"

"Chewed and swallowed," it repeated.

"What's that supposed to mean?" I asked.

"Explosion in three minutes thirty seconds," it boomed out.

"Sounds like a crossword clue. Do you do crosswords, Peter?" Tara asked.

"Not really," I replied.

We both fell silent, puzzling over the clue.

"T minus three minutes," the safe boomed.

"I've got it!" Tara suddenly burst out. "The answer's eight! Chewed and swallowed – is ate. Sounds like the number eight, you see."

"Brilliant!" the safe burst out. "Oops," it added, "I

shouldn't have said that."

"Well done, Tara," I said and Floppy jumped up and down in delight. Tara quickly pressed the number eight on the keypad.

"OK, OK," the safe said in a more composed voice. "Here's the second clue, but this one's a bit harder," it warned. "You eat it with custard or cream."

"You eat it with custard or cream," I repeated, puzzled. "Any ideas, Tara?"

"No," she replied. "I've just gone through all the numbers from zero to nine in my head. It doesn't make sense."

"T minus two minutes thirty seconds," the safe rang out.

I looked over to Floppy. "Don't ask me," he said despondently. "I don't eat custard or cream."

"Well, I do," I said, scratching my head. "With rhubarb crumble, and apple pie…that's it!" I cried.

"What is?" Tara said, looking rather confused.

"Pi. It's a special number in maths, 3.14."

I pressed the number three on the keypad but before I could find the decimal point the safe said, "Correct."

"Brilliant!" Floppy cried and fireworks burst above his head. "You did it, Peter!"

"All right, let's calm down shall we," the safe said sternly. "You haven't got the last clue yet, you know. Solve it and you'll have got the prize!"

"OK," we said, waiting expectantly for the clue.

"Well," the safe said impatiently.

"Well what?" I cried. "You haven't given us the clue yet!"

"Oh, yes, I have. And I'm not repeating it. Explosion in one minute ten seconds."

"You've given us the clue already?" I turned towards Tara in panic. "Can you remember what it said?"

"No, not exactly," she replied, "something about getting

a prize."

"Don't look at me," Floppy said meekly. "I don't remember either."

"T minus one minute!"

My mind went blank. I couldn't think. The safe was going to explode in one minute and I couldn't even remember the clue!

"Explosion in thirty seconds!" the safe warned.

"We're running out of time, Peter!" Tara cried.

"Got a prize, got a prize," I repeated desperately. "What could that mean? If you get a prize, you win a prize, but what's that got to do with numbers?"

"Explosion in ten seconds! Nine, eight…"

The final countdown had begun. We'd run out of time! I glanced at Tara and then at the door. We would have to make a run for it before the safe exploded.

"Got a prize, won a prize," Floppy suddenly cried. "The answer's one!"

Tara and I both dived for the keypad and pressed the number one at the same time.

"Correct," the safe boomed and its door sprang open. "Explosion sequence terminated."

"Well done, Floppy!" Tara said, blowing him a kiss. The little rabbit blushed in delight.

We all crowded round the safe, anxious to find out what it contained. I peered into the safe. There was a small envelope at the back. Tara reached in and took it out.

CHAPTER EIGHT

The Cave

The envelope was sealed with a small gold stamp.

"This isn't a diary!" Tara said in surprise.

"Hurry up, Tara! Open it!" Floppy cried, jumping up and down madly.

She opened the envelope carefully. Inside was a small plastic disk. She took it out and looked at it curiously.

"It's looks like a CD," she said, "only smaller. And there's some writing on it."

"What does it say?" I asked excitedly.

"*Diary volume XVI: the fourth dimension,*" she replied.

"That's Professor P's latest diary," Floppy said. "He always types it into his notebook computer and then saves it onto a CD."

I looked around the study. "There's no sign of a computer here," I said.

"His notebook computer is missing!" Floppy said in surprise. "Professor P must have taken it with him. We'll have to go to the basement and find a computer there."

We left the study and went down into the basement. Floppy led us to the room called *Complex Computers*. The floor and all the surfaces were piled high with rather old and battered looking computers. We searched through them and found a newer one. I switched the computer on and it hummed into life. I put the disk inside.

"I am afraid I am not working properly," it said and promptly shut down.

We tried another computer. It coughed and spluttered, then switched itself off.

"We'll never find one that works!" Floppy said, annoyed.

After two more failed attempts we finally found a computer that worked. I put the disk into the drive and an image of Professor P appeared on the screen.

"This is a complete record of my research into the fourth dimension. Click on the links below for video and/or text information."

"The fourth dimension?" Tara said, puzzled. "What's that?"

"I don't know," I replied as I clicked on one of the links.

We waited excitedly as a window popped up on the screen and loaded a video file. I clicked the play button and a small image of Professor P appeared.

"He looks so young!" I exclaimed.

"And look at those trousers!" Tara giggled.

The video showed Professor P in a small lecture theatre talking to a group of about twenty people, most of them older than he was. A caption at the bottom of the screen read *Department of Applied Mathematics and Theoretical Physics, Cambridge University*. Professor P was talking excitedly and scribbling mathematical equations on the black board.

"Do you know what it means?" Tara asked, turning to Floppy.

Floppy scratched his head, turned upside down and tried to read it. "No," he said as he flipped the right way up, "I've no idea."

I fast-forwarded the video.

"So, in conclusion," Professor P continued, "I have shown that non-causality is possible within the framework of General Relativity. Are there any questions?"

There was a brief round of applause and then an old man sitting at the back of the room spoke.

"Professor P," he said, "are we correct in believing that your theoretical analysis has just proved..." he paused, "that time travel may be possible?"

"Yes, Dr Johnson," Professor P replied slowly and clearly. "That is correct."

"Time travel!" I cried out in amazement. "I thought that was just science fiction!"

Tara stared at me, unable to speak.

"What else does it say?" Floppy asked impatiently.

I scrolled down through the pages of dates and clicked on the last one. It was dated Tuesday, the last time we had seen Professor P.

After Floppy's attempt to make a metal detector this afternoon I realised his program has again become unstable. I have therefore completed a new program for Floppy, called Superbrain 4.0, which should fix his memory leak problem. No time to test it now. Will load and debug it when I return on Thursday morning.

This morning I took all the equipment to the site and began construction of the pyramid.

I stopped reading and looked up at Tara.

"Do you remember when we met Professor P on the beach, on Tuesday afternoon?" I asked excitedly.

"Yes," Tara nodded. "He was carrying that heavy rucksack and Sleepy was weighed down with all his tools."

"He must have been setting up an experiment somewhere!" I said.

"Hurry up, Peter!" Floppy urged. "Read on!"

I read out the rest of the diary entry, *"Later tonight, when the tide is out, I will return to the cave."*

Floppy suddenly cried out in horror, "That's why Professor P hasn't returned! He's had an accident in a cave! He's slipped and hurt himself. He's lying there unconscious or dead!"

"But where…?" I began.

"There's a cave in the cliffs," Floppy replied. "We must find it!"

Floppy rushed over to the door. "Hurry!" he cried.

We quickly climbed up the spiral staircase, called Sparky and Sleepy and left the house. We ran up the footpath to the cliffs as fast as we could and scrambled down the steps to the beach.

"This way," I said, pointing to the right. "Professor P was coming from over there when we met him."

As we struggled along the pebbles a strong wind blew in from the sea. Floppy coughed a few times and a red scarf appeared around his neck. We came to the end of the beach. I stopped and looked at the large boulders blocking the way.

"You have to climb over the rocks!" Floppy urged. "The cave is on the other side."

Sleepy jumped up onto the rocks and barked. Sparky scrambled up after her. Tara and I climbed up cautiously onto the slippery boulders. Salty spray blew into our faces from the waves crashing onto the rocks below.

"Peter, caves!" Tara cried out.

I looked up and saw a small cove. At the far end were three caves cut into the base of the cliff. Sleepy jumped down off the rocks and ran over to the largest cave.

We climbed down onto the sand and then ran over to the cave. The opening was small and I had to bend my head to avoid hitting it on the narrow roof. Once inside I could hear the echoing sound of dripping water.

"Spooky, isn't it?" Tara whispered.

I nodded. "And it's so dark. I wish we'd brought a torch."

"You want light?" Floppy said. He glowed brightly and the cave was filled with pale pink light.

"Thanks, Floppy," I said as we walked deeper into the cave.

Drips of water fell down on our heads and splashed in puddles on the sand. Sleepy barked and the loud noise echoed around the cave. We followed her as she ran to the back of the cave. The cave narrowed and led up onto a rocky ledge.

"Where's Sleepy?" I cried suddenly. "She's gone!"

I peered into the dark shadows at the back of the cave. There was no sign of the big dog – she had completely disappeared! Out of the darkness I heard the muffled sound of her barking. Sparky ran towards the noise and he disappeared too!

"Peter, over there!" Tara cried, pointing to a shadow on the wall.

We rushed over and found a dark hole in the rock, about a metre wide.

"A tunnel!" I exclaimed.

"I'll go in first," Floppy said, darting into the tunnel.

Tara followed closely behind. I got down onto my hands and knees and crawled in.

"Yuck!" I cried as my knee sank into a pile of cold wet slippery seaweed.

THE CAVE

As I crawled along the narrow passageway it gradually began to curve upwards and I wondered when it would end. The light quickly began to fade as Floppy raced ahead of us. Then, out of the darkness, came a chilling howl. "Noooo…"

"Floppy! What is it?" I called out. "Have you found Professor P?"

Tara and I scrambled up the tunnel as quickly as we could. My heart was pounding. What had Floppy found? Was Professor P badly hurt? Was he still alive?

We burst out of the tunnel into a small cave. There was no sign of Professor P, just a large hollow pyramid, glowing faintly and casting an eerie yellow light onto the cave walls.

"What is it?" Tara cried as we stood and stared at the strange object in the middle of the cave.

"I don't know," I replied.

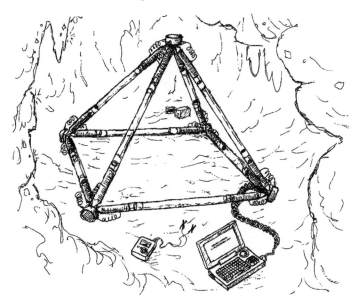

"Careful!" Floppy called out as we walked over to the pyramid to take a closer look.

As I got closer to the pyramid I heard a faint humming sound and saw that the sides were made of tubes filled with a glowing liquid. Tara reached out to touch one of the tubes. As her hand got closer to the tube her hair began to stand on end.

"Don't touch it," Floppy cried. "It's high voltage!"

Tara quickly pulled her hand away.

We walked round the pyramid. A notebook computer was lying next to it on the cave floor. It was attached to the pyramid with a bundle of coloured wires. I knelt down and peered at the computer screen.

"Temporal functions calibrated. Final sequence completed," I read out.

"What does that mean?" Tara asked, puzzled.

"Something terrible has happened," Floppy cried, pulling his long ears over his eyes and shaking his head. "That's what it means!"

CHAPTER NINE

Superbrain

"What's happened, Floppy?" I asked urgently.

"The pyramid…" he stopped. "It's a…"

"What?"

"It's a…" he shook his head.

"There's no sign of an accident, Floppy," Tara said.

Floppy nodded. "True," he sniffed.

"I'm sure Professor P is all right," she added kindly. "It looks like he just set up one of his experiments here in the cave and left it running."

"I hope so," Floppy said.

"There's nothing more we can do here," I said. "Let's go back to the house now."

As we left the cave I turned back and looked at the strange pyramid. What did it do, I wondered? Why had Professor P been so secretive about it? Why had he hidden it in the cave? It was all *very* mysterious.

We crawled through the tunnel and out into the main cave. When we reached the entrance a large wave splashed into the cave. We went outside onto the beach and I saw how quickly the tide had come in. We ran across the sand, dodging the incoming waves, and climbed over the rocks.

I felt a drop of rain and glanced up at the sky. The fine weather of the past few weeks had finally changed. Dark rain clouds were gathering overhead. I shivered in my thin T-shirt as a cold wind blew in from the sea.

When we arrived at Professor P's house there was still no sign of him.

I glanced at my watch. "It's one o'clock," I said. "Let's go back to my house for lunch, Tara."

"Good idea," she agreed. "Floppy can stay here and ring

71

us when Professor P gets home."

"Bye, Floppy," we called as we left the house. "See you soon."

But Floppy did not reply. He had been unusually quiet all the way back from the caves and now he was completely lost in his own thoughts. Something had obviously started him thinking!

After lunch Tara and I played on my computer while we waited to hear from Professor P.

Finally, at three thirty, the phone rang.

"That'll be him," I said, jumping up from the computer. I dashed down the stairs into the hallway and picked up the phone.

"Professor P?" I said hopefully.

But no, it was Floppy who replied. "Oh, Peter, thank goodness it's you! You must come round straight away. There's something I've got to show you, it's very, very important."

"What is it?" I replied.

"I know where Professor P has gone," he said almost in tears. "And why he hasn't come back. Oh, it's terrible, Peter, terrible…"

"What…"

"You must come now!" he interrupted and hung up.

Tara was standing at the top of the stairs. "Was that Professor P?" she asked.

"No, it was Floppy," I replied, "and he's really upset."

I told Tara what he had said. She leapt down the stairs two at a time. I called Sparky in from the garden and we ran all the way to Professor P's house. We arrived panting and breathless ten minutes later. Floppy was waiting for us in the hallway. He had a look of desperation on his face.

"I know what's happened to Professor P," he cried. "Follow me."

Tara looked at me anxiously as Floppy led us up the

stairs. He pointed to a door and said, "Go in there, into Professor P's bedroom."

Tara went first and cried out in horror. I quickly followed her. The room looked as though it had been turned upside down! The drawers in the bedside cabinet were open; clothes had been taken out of the wardrobe and dumped over the floor; the sheets had been roughly pulled from the bed.

"Someone's broken in," Tara cried in dismay. "It's been completely ransacked!"

"We'd better call the police," I said, moving towards the door.

"There's no need for that," Floppy said impatiently, shaking his head. "It always looks like this."

"What!" Tara exclaimed in disbelief.

"And I thought my room was messy!" I chuckled.

"I brought you here to show you something else," Floppy said seriously. "Look, over there on the bedside table."

We went over to the table. On it was an open book and a spiral bound notebook.

"It's a book about fossils," Tara said as she picked it up. "Is that what you wanted to show us, Floppy."

"Read the notebook," he urged.

I picked up the notebook and tried to read the small spidery handwriting.

"It's really difficult to make out," I said, "but I think it says *Ichthyosaurs should not present any danger, but will take electro*...it looks like *electroprod, in case they should attack.* And at the bottom of the page there's a list."

"Let's have a look," Tara said curiously.

"Essential items to acquire," she read out. *"Underwater camera, diving equipment, inflatable dinghy."*

"There!" Floppy said. "Now, do you understand?"

We looked at him blankly.

73

"Professor P has…" Floppy stopped and a look of terror appeared on his face.

"Has what, Floppy?" Tara asked gently.

"He's gone back in time!" Floppy burst out. "Professor P has gone back 150 million years into the past."

Tara and I stared at Floppy, speechless!

"I've worked it all out," he continued. "Remember that video clip we saw in the basement? Professor P was giving a lecture and said that time travel was possible."

"Well, it might be possible, but that doesn't mean…" I began.

"And the pyramid in the cave," Floppy interrupted. "I know what it is now. It's a…" he stopped. "It's a time machine!"

"A time machine!" Tara and I cried out together.

"Yes," Floppy nodded, "Professor P's notebook," he paused to blow his nose, "and all the research he was doing, the notes he made, the equipment he needed…"

Floppy broke down, too distressed to continue.

I picked the notebook up again and looked at it more closely. At the bottom of one of the pages was a small doodle of a pyramid. I read out, *"The best time to go is the late Jurassic, 150 million years ago. I should be able to get some excellent shots of the extinct sea reptiles."*

I glanced up at Tara and saw a look of shock on her face. "Professor P *was* planning a trip back in time," I said slowly.

"And that's where he is now," Floppy cried out hysterically. "But it's all gone horribly wrong."

"Why?" Tara asked.

"Professor P can't return!" he replied.

"What!" I exclaimed.

"He can't come back," Floppy said, sobbing loudly.

"That doesn't make sense, Floppy!" I said. "Professor P wouldn't go back in time without being able to return home."

"But he didn't mean to!" Floppy cried. "The time machine went wrong! It should have gone with him but it didn't. It's still here in the cave. Professor P is trapped in the past with no way of getting back!"

I couldn't believe what I was hearing. Surely Floppy was wrong. I picked up the notebook again and read it more carefully. There was no doubt that Professor P was planning to go back in time. He'd gone to the cave on Tuesday evening and still hadn't returned three days later. But could the pyramid in the cave really be a time machine?

"What if Floppy's right?" Tara said eventually, breaking the silence. "What can we do?"

"I think we've got to get help," I said.

"No!" Floppy cried. "There is only one thing we can do. We have to fix the time machine and send it to Professor P so he can come back."

"Fix it!" I exclaimed. "But how? We don't even know how it works. We couldn't possible fix it."

"I can," he replied quietly.

I looked at Tara doubtfully and she shook her head.

"I know you mean well, Floppy," she said kindly, "and you really want to help Professor P, but…"

"I *can* do it," he insisted.

"But, Floppy," I began, not knowing quite how to continue. "Well, remember the time when you tried to help us build the metal detector and…"

"That was different," Floppy interrupted. "That was before. Now Professor P has finished my new program, Superbrain 4.0. He told me all about it and said it would make me really, really clever. So when the new program is loaded into my memory I'll be able to fix the time machine."

He looked at us pleadingly. "We have to do this or

Professor P will be lost forever."

"It might work," I said hopefully as I remembered Professor P's diary entry about Superbrain 4.0. "If we could find the program we might be able to load it."

With a sudden burst of energy Floppy sprouted wings, flew out of the bedroom and down the stairs. We ran after him and followed him to the door leading down into the basement.

"Stay here, Sparky, you too, Sleepy, we'll be back soon," I said, closing the door.

We went down the stairs into the basement and back to the *Complex Computers* room. I opened the door and we went inside.

"The program's in there," Floppy said, pointing to a filing cabinet.

I opened the top drawer, found a section called *Perfect Programs* and took out a disk with *Superbrain 4.0* written on it.

"That's it!" Floppy cried in delight. "Put the disk in that computer over there and put my sphere next to it, next to the infrared port. I'll do the rest."

I started the computer and inserted the disk. A box appeared on the screen with the message *Connecting to remote device. Please wait.* A moment later another box appeared saying *Transferring Superbrain 4.0 to remote device.*

Floppy disappeared and we waited nervously for the transfer to complete. Ten minutes later a message popped up on the screen *Transfer successful. Please tap sphere twice to start program.*

"Let's hope it worked," I said nervously, tapping Floppy's sphere. Nothing happened. I tapped the sphere again. Hundreds of lines of tiny mathematical symbols appeared, floating in the air above the sphere.

"Floppy! Are you there?" Tara called out.

"I am Superbrain," said a lifeless computer voice.

"What are you doing?" I asked, staring at the streams of mathematical symbols and equation.

"I am working on the Grand Unification Theory, also know as the Theory of Everything. I am currently modifying parameters in M-Theory to…"

"But where's Floppy?" Tara asked.

Superbrain was silent for a moment and then replied. "The program you call Floppy is unnecessary for String Theory. No other tasks can be run until this process has finished. Therefore Floppy has been terminated."

"What!" I cried.

"Terminated!" Tara exclaimed. "We didn't want him terminated."

"Do you wish to terminate current program and reinitialise Superbrain 3.01?" it asked coldly.

"Well…" Tara hesitated. "Not exactly. We want Floppy back but…"

"We need him to be clever," I interrupted. "Can you upgrade him?"

"As you wish," the computer replied. "I can apply a patch to the old program. It should substantially improve its performance but the resulting program may be slightly unstable."

"Unstable?" Tara said. "I don't like the sound of that!"

"Nor do I," I added, "but we need Floppy to be clever so he can fix the time machine."

"We have to try," Tara said.

"All right," I agreed. "Go ahead, computer!"

"Recompiling…" it said and the lines of mathematical equations disappeared.

We waited in silence for what seemed like ages.

"I hope the program hasn't crashed," I said nervously.

Five minutes later a loud popping sound filled the room. A large grey owl appeared above the desk.

77

"Floppy?" I asked. "Is that you?"

The owl looked around, its head turning in a complete circle.

"I think," he hesitated. "I think it is." He looked curiously at himself. He gradually faded and then disappeared completely.

"Floppy!" Tara called out.

The owl reappeared, slightly fuzzy at the edges.

"I feel rather strange," he said and his body disappeared leaving only his head.

He disappeared completely and then reappeared upside down.

"Egnarts leef I," he said, "egnarts yrev!"

He flipped himself over and shook himself vigorously. "Ah, that's better," he added.

"Are you all right now, Floppy?" Tara asked.

"All right," he said. "I'm more than all right. I am the greatest intelligence in the world. I am SuperFloppy!"

Tara giggled.

"So you can fix the time machine?" I asked hopefully.

"Fix it? Of course, I can fix it!" he replied. "It will be a trivial matter. Take me to it and I will begin work immediately."

"Yes!" we cried, jumping up in delight.

I picked up Floppy's sphere and we raced out of the room and up the spiral stairs. Sparky and Sleepy greeted us enthusiastically as we went into the kitchen.

"We're going to rescue Professor P!" Tara said excitedly as she stroked Sleepy.

"Come on, Sparky," I cried, "let's go!"

As we left the house the front door called out after us, "Good luck!"

When we got to the caves Sparky and Sleepy ran inside first. I told them to wait in the main cave while we made our way through the tunnel to the time machine. I didn't want them getting in the way and distracting Floppy.

When we were inside the smaller cave I put Floppy's sphere next to the notebook computer by the pyramid. A message appeared on the screen. It read *Computers connected. Transferring data.*

We waited anxiously to discover what Floppy would learn from the computer. Had Professor P really gone back in time? Was he trapped in the past? Could Floppy fix the time machine? Would we be able to rescue Professor P?

CHAPTER TEN

Preparations

I glanced at my watch impatiently. We had been in the cave for nearly quarter of an hour. Why was Floppy taking so long? Tara looked nervously at me.

"Floppy?" I said finally.

"Yes, Peter," the owl replied slowly.

"Any news?" I asked.

"No, not yet."

As we waited I sat and watched strange shadows cast by the glowing tubes dance across the cave walls. Finally Floppy looked up at us. He had a very serious expression on his face.

"Professor P has indeed been sent back alone into the past," he said grimly. "He made a mistake in the software and this caused him to go back without the time machine."

"No!" Tara exclaimed.

"He has gone back 150 million years," Floppy said, "to the Jurassic Period, just as I suspected."

Tara and I stared at each other in horror, not quite able to make sense of the terrible news.

"Can you fix the problem, Floppy?" I asked quietly.

"I will see," he said, turning back to the computer and shutting his eyes.

We waited again. I felt quite sick in my stomach now. I was stunned by the news. I stared at Floppy, not daring to take my eyes off him, desperately hoping he would succeed. Ten minutes later he opened his eyes and turned to us.

"I can fix the problem," he said, "but it's not easy. It will take some time."

"How long?" I asked anxiously.

"Fourteen hours, twenty nine minutes and fifteen seconds."

I looked at my watch.

"It's nearly five o'clock," I said. "Adding on fourteen and a half hours will make it…"

"Approximately seven thirty tomorrow morning," Floppy answered.

"We'd better go home," Tara said. "We can't stay here till then. We'll come back in the morning, Floppy."

"Good idea," he said. "You can use the time to get ready."

"Get ready?" I said, puzzled. "What for?"

"For the trip," Floppy replied.

"What trip?" Tara asked, confused.

"The trip back in time," Floppy continued.

Tara laughed. "Oh, Floppy," she said kindly. "Don't be silly. *We're* not going back in time."

I laughed too. "I think you're getting a bit mixed up again, Floppy," I said nervously. "You're just going to fix the time machine and send *it* back in time to Professor P so he can come home."

"No, Peter," Floppy said firmly. He was now beginning to sound quite irritated. "I have everything quite correct. The time machine cannot go back on its own. We will all need to return to the past with it to rescue Professor P."

"Why?" I exclaimed.

Floppy sighed and said, as if it were obvious, "Because we will have to find him."

"Find him?" I repeated.

"Yes," Floppy replied. "Due to the uncertainty principle it will not be possible to send the time machine back to the exact time and place Professor P went to, so you will need to go and find him."

"But…" I stammered.

He ignored me and continued, "You will need enough

food and water for two days."

"Two days!" Tara burst out.

"Yes," he replied. "That should be sufficient."

Tara looked at me, her mouth open in astonishment.

"Floppy," she said, shaking her head. "You don't understand. We can't go away for that long. Our parents would never let us go!"

"But they don't need to know," he said. "I'll set the time co-ordinates for us to return one minute after we have left."

He saw our puzzled looks and continued, "You'll be two days in the past but will return just after you left. So it will seem as though you've only been gone for a minute."

"But, Floppy," Tara protested, "we can't go back in time. It's too dangerous!"

I nodded in agreement. "We don't even know if the time machine will work properly this time."

"It *will* work correctly," Floppy said confidently.

"But what about dinosaurs…" Tara started.

"Professor P would not have chosen to go back to the Jurassic if it was dangerous," Floppy interrupted. "He knew what he was doing. He studied the period carefully."

"But…" I began.

"No buts," Floppy said firmly. "We do not have time. The calibration is already beginning to drift. We have to go as soon as I have corrected the program."

I did not know what to say.

Floppy broke the silence. "We must go," he said, his voice shaking. "If we don't Professor P will never be able to return. He will be lost in time forever. We must go tomorrow!"

I looked at Tara.

"I don't think we've got any choice, Peter!" she said slowly.

We left Floppy to work on the time machine and crawled into the tunnel. When we reached the main cave

Sleepy and Sparky ran towards us barking madly. We walked slowly in the dim light towards the cave entrance and then out into the bright sunlight. Sleepy and Sparky ran off to play in the sea. Tara and I sat down on the beach. Neither of us spoke for a few minutes. Tara broke the silence.

"It doesn't seem possible, does it?" she said.

"No," I replied. "I can hardly believe it. A time machine in the cave. Professor P trapped in the past. And we're going back to rescue him!"

"I wonder what it will be like when we get there?" she asked nervously. "Do you think it will be really hot?"

"I've no idea," I replied, shaking my head. "It might be. We'd better take plenty of drinking water with us just in case."

"And what about dinosaurs?" she added. "Do you think it will be safe?"

"Floppy said it would be," I replied, "but…"

"We've got to find out for ourselves, Peter," Tara said, standing up quickly.

I nodded in agreement.

"We could start by looking in my encyclopaedias," she continued, "but there's not much detail in them, I'm afraid."

"We need an expert," I said thoughtfully.

"I know!" Tara said brightly. "Let's ask Mary. I'm sure she'll be able to tell us."

"Good idea!" I said, jumping up. "Let's go and see her right now."

I called to the Sparky and Sleepy and we hurried off to the village. When we arrived at the Fossil Shop Mary greeted us warmly.

"Tara, Peter and Sparky, how nice to see you. And who's this?" she said, pointing to Sleepy.

"She's called Sleepy," Tara said. "She belongs to a

friend of ours, we're looking after her while he's away."

"She's very friendly," Mary said, stroking Sleepy on the head. "Have you come to bring me some more fossils?"

"No, not today," Tara replied. "We...er...we came to ask you something."

Mary looked at us questioningly.

"We need to know *exactly* what it was like 150 million years ago," Tara continued.

"Oh, is that all," Mary said with a sigh of relief. "I thought something had happened, from the worried look on your faces!"

"Oh, no!" I said quickly, glancing at Tara. "We need to help a friend..."

"Well, you've come at a good time," Mary said, glancing at the clock. "I don't think I'm going to get any more customers now – I might as well close the shop for the day."

Mary put the closed sign on the door and locked it. She put a bowl of water on the floor for Sparky and Sleepy, which they lapped eagerly, before lying down by the door.

Tara and I followed Mary into the back room. She took a book from one of the shelves and we all sat down on the chairs by the window to look at it.

"150 million years ago," she said, opening the book, "was the end of the Jurassic Period. It was the time when the great dinosaurs ruled the land."

"What sort of dinosaurs?" I asked.

"Herds of giant sauropods grazed the land," Mary replied, turning to a picture. "Some weighed more than 70 tonnes – that's more than 20 fully grown elephants, and at over 45 metres in length they could flatten a house with one swing of their tails."

Tara looked pale. "Not very friendly then?" she said meekly.

"I don't think friendly is quite the right word, Tara!"

Mary chuckled. "But being vegetarians they wouldn't try to eat you!"

We sighed with relief.

"But," Mary continued, "there were plenty of gigantic carnivores only too happy to eat them! At 12 metres long an allosaurus could finish one off pretty quickly."

"12 metres!" I cried.

"Yes, and weighing in at 3 tonnes, it was quite a heavyweight. But it could still move at lightning speeds and you certainly wouldn't want to get anywhere near its huge claws or razor sharp teeth."

I gulped in horror.

Mary looked up from the book. "There's no need to look so worried, Peter!" she laughed. "They are extinct, you know."

"Oh, yes," I said, smiling weakly.

"You wouldn't find any in this area in the Jurassic Period though, they only lived on the mainland."

"Oh?" I said surprised. "So what was it like here then?"

"It was a shallow sea full of coral reefs and small islands," she replied. "It was warm and sunny, a bit of a tropical paradise, in fact."

"Sounds great!" Tara said cheerfully. "So it would be safe?"

"Yes," Mary replied. "You'd be perfectly safe on the islands. The big dinosaurs weren't good swimmers and they didn't like to cross the sea because of the dangerous creatures lurking in the depths."

"Best not to go for a swim then," I joked.

Mary laughed, "Definitely not!"

She leafed through her book and found the chapter on sea creatures. "This chapter shows what it was like here in the Jurassic Period," she explained

"How do scientists know so much about the past?" I asked Mary as I glanced at the pictures.

"By studying rocks and the fossils they find in them," she replied. "But they don't know exactly what the animals were like because the fossils usually only show the bones and shells. They have to make some good guesses too. Most scientists would love the chance to see a real prehistoric creature and find out if they're right!"

Tara and I glanced at each other knowingly.

"Here," Mary said, giving us the book. "Why don't you have a look at the pictures while I close up the shop and empty the till?"

Mary left the room and Tara and I turned the pages eagerly. The book was full of beautiful pictures of the deep blue sea dotted with small emerald coloured islands. It looked more like a brochure for an exotic holiday than a book on fossils!

The book had pictures of brightly coloured fish and squid swimming in the sea and huge birds with long pointed beaks skimming over the surface of the water. As we looked at the pictures of all the creatures that lived 150 million years ago I began to feel more excited at the idea of our journey.

Mary returned a few minutes later. "Well, I'm ready to go home now," she said. "I hope I've been of some help to you but if you need to find out more you could have a look on the Internet, check out the Jurassic Coast web sites."

"OK," I said happily.

"And you can borrow this fossil book if you like," Mary added as we got up. "I've got another copy."

"Thanks, Mary," Tara added.

"You're most welcome," she replied.

I put Sparky on the lead, we said goodbye to Mary and left the shop. As we walked up the hill towards the estate we chatted excitedly about what Mary had told us. I felt much happier about going back in time now. It seemed as though we would be in no danger from dinosaurs and as long as we kept out of the sea we would be completely safe.

When we got back to my house we went up to my room to look at Mary's book in more detail. We turned to the chapter on sea creatures again and started to read it carefully.

"Isn't it beautiful?" Tara said as we gazed at the pictures of the islands.

"Yes," I replied, looking at all the brightly coloured sea creatures. "It says here that ammonites were one of the commonest animals living in the sea."

We turned to the next page and saw a picture of an ichthyosaurus. It was rather like a dolphin but with larger eyes and a long smiling snout.

"Looks friendly enough," I commented.

"Apart from those teeth!" Tara added, pointing to the long rows of sharp teeth.

My mother called up to say that my tea was ready.

"I better go home now," Tara said, glancing at her watch. "Then I'll start packing."

"OK," I said. "I'll have a look on the Internet after tea and come round to show you what I've found."

"Good idea, see you later," Tara said as she got up to leave.

After tea I went back to my room to look on the Internet. I found the Jurassic Coast web sites first and then clicked on the links to the other fossil sites. I printed out all the useful information and pictures I could find. When I had finished I hurriedly packed my rucksack with a change of clothes and a thin sleeping bag, then went round to Tara's house. We went up to her bedroom and she closed the door behind us.

"I'm almost finished packing," she said, picking up a large piece of paper. "Clothes, water, sleeping bag, toothbrush, toothpaste, sun cream…"

I looked at all the neat piles of clothes on the bed.

"Tara! You're not taking *all* this stuff are you," I cried in amazement.

"No," she laughed. "That's my washing, mum's just brought it up for me to put away."

"Well, that's a relief," I laughed.

"Now, where was I?" she said. "Oh, yes, toothpaste, sun cream, sketch pad, towels, games…"

"Games!" I exclaimed.

"For the evenings," she explained. "We don't want to get bored."

"I don't think we'll get bored, Tara!"

She put the list down and turned to me with a smile. "Did you find out anything useful from the Internet, Peter?"

"I tried to find out if there's anything we can eat on the islands," I said. "I thought there might be coconuts or bananas…"

"And?" she eagerly.

"Unfortunately there weren't any," I replied. "There weren't any flowering plants in the Jurassic Period, so I don't think there'll be any fruits."

"Oh, well, I guess we'd better pack enough food for the whole two days," she said, jotting a note on her list.

"I found some more pictures of the sea creatures," I said, giving her the printouts from the web sites. "Look at this one. It's called a liopleurodon."

"Looks harmless enough," she said, glancing at the page.

"Harmless!" I cried. "Tara, they were gigantic, the biggest carnivores ever to have lived. Here's another picture of one with its mouth open. Look at those teeth. And its skull is five metres long."

"Five metres!" she exclaimed, looking rather shocked. "What did they eat?"

"Anything they felt like I expect," I replied.

She laughed, then looked at me nervously. "I really don't like the idea of meeting one of those."

"I did find out something else," I said, clearing my throat. "One of the web sites said that, very occasionally, some of the smaller dinosaurs did cross to the islands."

"How small?" Tara asked, worried.

"I don't know, it didn't say, but they were scavengers," I added quickly. "They didn't actually kill for themselves, they just combed the beaches looking for dead animals to eat."

"Yuck!" she said, screwing up her face.

"Let's hope we don't meet one," I said nervously.

We spent the next half hour packing our rucksacks and checking we had everything we would need.

"Well, that's it, everything's packed," Tara sighed as we slumped down onto the floor. "We're all ready to go!"

CHAPTER ELEVEN

Help!

The alarm clock woke me with a start early the next morning. I rubbed the sleep from my eyes, hurriedly washed, dressed and went downstairs to feed Sleepy and Sparky. I wrote a note to my parents to tell them that Tara and I were going to the beach before the tide came in. At exactly seven o'clock there was a knock on the back door. It was Tara.

"Hi, Peter, are you ready?" she asked.

"Yes, all set," I replied, picking up my rucksack.

I called to Sparky and Sleepy and we all left the house quietly.

"Did you have any breakfast?" Tara asked.

"No, I didn't have time."

"I made some toast and chocolate spread sandwiches," she said. "Do you want some?"

"Er, no, thanks," I replied politely.

"I'm not really hungry either," she said. "We can save them for later, when we're back in time."

Back in time! Were we really about to set off on a journey, 150 million years in the past? I could feel a hard knot of tension in my stomach. Yesterday the trip had seemed like an exciting adventure, but now I was not quite so sure.

As we reached the end of the road leading out of the estate I turned to look back at my house. Would I ever see it again? We could still turn back, I thought, it wasn't too late. Tara glanced back too and I could see she was thinking the same.

Sparky tugged at his lead, pulling me down the hill. We walked down the hill towards the beach in silence. When

90

we arrived at the car park I let Sparky off his lead and he and Sleepy ran down onto the beach. Tara and I walked slowly along the pebbles towards the caves.

"Do you think Floppy will have fixed the time machine?" I asked.

"I..." she hesitated. "I hope so. He seemed very sure about it yesterday."

We walked on again in silence. It was such a calm day; I could hear the gentle sound of waves lapping on the beach and seagulls crying in the distance. But I felt far from calm though.

"I wonder what the journey through time will be like," Tara said nervously. "Do you think we'll just suddenly disappear from here and reappear in the past?"

"I don't know," I replied quietly.

We climbed over the rocks and headed over to the caves. As we approached, Tara took out her torch. We walked through the cold damp cave to the tunnel at the back. Tara went into the tunnel first, followed by Sleepy and Sparky. I climbed in after them.

As we came out into the smaller cave I saw Floppy floating above the pyramid.

"Peter, Tara, you're here at last," he said. "Everything is ready. Let's go."

"So you've fixed the time machine, Floppy?" I asked apprehensively.

"I have recalculated the Quantum equations and rewritten the appropriate algorithms," he replied.

"And we can go back in time and rescue Professor P?" Tara asked.

"Yes, yes, now get inside and we'll go," he said, guiding us towards the pyramid. "The sooner we leave the better. Hurry up, please."

"Are you sure it's safe, Floppy?" I asked as Tara moved towards the pyramid.

"Yes, completely safe," he replied. "The journey back in time will be almost instantaneous. The actual transfer will take place in less than a tenth of a second. You won't feel a thing! Now, into the pyramid, please."

Tara and I sat down in the pyramid. Sparky jumped inside and looked at me questioningly, wondering what strange game we were playing. Sleepy sniffed the tubes suspiciously and after a little persuasion, sat down in the pyramid, resting her head on Tara's knee.

"Hold on tightly to the tubes," Floppy said. "And Peter, you hold onto the notebook computer. When you're ready press the enter key to begin the initialisation sequence."

I picked up the computer and looked at Tara. She nodded. I pressed the key.

"Countdown begun!" the computer said in a loud voice.

The tubes started to glow and hum faintly. The noise suddenly increased and the whole pyramid started to vibrate.

I gripped a tube with one hand and the notebook computer with the other. My heart began to race and my hand tensed around the tube in readiness for the journey.

The tubes flickered and began to glow more brightly, then suddenly gave out a bright flash of light. Sleepy jumped up startled. She barked and ran out of the pyramid.

"Sleepy! Come back!" I yelled.

She barked again, dived into the tunnel and disappeared out of the cave. I leapt up out of the pyramid and went after her.

"Leave her, Peter!" Floppy cried. "Get back in the time machine! The initialisation sequence only takes three minutes. I can't stop it now it's begun."

"We can't go without her," I called as I crawled into the tunnel. "We need her to help us find Professor P."

"Oh, hurry, Peter!" Tara shouted anxiously.

I scrambled down the narrow tunnel calling out to Sleepy. I caught up with her in the main cave and grabbed hold of her collar.

"Come on, Sleepy," I urged. "You've got to come with us."

I tried to lead her back towards the tunnel but she pulled away from me.

"Please, Sleepy!" I pleaded. "We need your help to find Professor P!"

"Woof!" she barked on hearing Professor P's name. I led her back to the tunnel. She went in first and I followed closely behind. I had almost reached the small cave when a brilliant flash of yellow light filled the tunnel.

I rushed to the end of the tunnel and gasped in horror when I got to the cave. There was no sign of Tara, Sparky or Floppy. They had completely disappeared. All that filled the cave was a fading yellow glow from the tubes of the time machine.

I ran over to the notebook computer. A message written

in big red letters flashed on the screen. *Successful transfer to time co-ordinate: 01 Jan 150,000,000BC*. I stared at it in disbelief!

"No!" I cried out in horror.

Sleepy ran up to the pyramid and barked at it loudly. She looked at me, as if to say, "What's happened? Where are Tara and Sparky?"

"They've gone, Sleepy!" I cried. "They've gone without us!"

I stared at the empty pyramid in dismay.

"Oh, Sleepy," I cried, slumping down onto the cave floor. "This can't be happening!"

I sat motionless, listening to the faint hum from the tubes, too shocked to move. Floppy hadn't fixed the time machine – it was still here! Professor P, Tara, Sparky and Floppy were all lost in the past with no way of coming back.

I don't know how long I sat staring at the empty pyramid, but it felt like hours. My body was cold and stiff from sitting in the damp cave and I realised I needed to move. I could not stay in the cave any longer, I had to go and get help. I rose unsteadily to my feet. Sleepy jumped up and licked my hands gently.

I walked slowly to the tunnel entrance. Sleepy followed me and went into the tunnel first. I crawled down after her, feeling my way slowly in the darkness. We reached the main cave and went out into the sunlight. The bright light blinded me at first, my eyes used to the darkness of the cave. I sat down on the rocks and waited for my eyes to adjust.

I tried to decide what to do. First I would have to go home and tell my parents everything…

"No way!" I cried. I couldn't possibly tell them the truth! They would never believe me! How could I tell them about the time machine and that we were going back in time to rescue Professor P on the advice of a holographic rabbit! And now that Tara and Sparky had disappeared too…

I buried my head in my hands. There had to be another way. I tried to concentrate but my mind was in a whirl. All I could think about was Tara, Sparky and Professor P. What was I to do? If only I could fix the time machine, I thought, then I could go back and rescue them. But that was impossible – if Floppy had failed, how could I ever hope to fix it? No, there was only one thing I could do – I would just have to go home and tell my parents what had happened.

I stood up despondently and walked along the beach with Sleepy at my heels. As we came to the steps in the cliff leading up to Professor P's house she ran ahead and waited by them.

"This way, Sleepy," I said, walking past the steps. "We're going to my house."

Sleepy barked and ran up the steps. I ran after her.

"No, Sleepy, we're not going to Professor P's house," I said, gently catching hold of her collar.

As I spoke I suddenly had an idea. I remembered the video diary we had found in Professor P's basement. He had been giving a lecture to the Cambridge professors. Perhaps he had told one of them about his time machine and explained how it worked. Perhaps one of them would know how to fix it! If I could find a phone number from the diary I could call and ask for help.

"That's it!" I cried excitedly. "Change of plan, Sleepy. We *are* going to Professor P's house!"

We sprinted along the footpath, through the fields and into the woods. When we arrived at the house Sleepy ran in through the side gate to the back door. It was unlocked so I opened it and went into the kitchen and through to the hallway.

"Stay here, Sleepy," I said, opening the door to the basement. "I'll be back soon."

"Woof, woof," she barked urgently.

I shut the door behind me and hurried down the rickety old stairs. I walked quickly down the long corridor towards the *Complex Computers* room and went inside. I turned on the computer we had used before and waited for the diary to appear on the screen. Nothing happened. I checked the disk drive. The disk was missing! I was sure we had left it in the computer. I searched everywhere, through all the cupboards, under files, even in the wastepaper bin. It was gone!

"Oh, where is it?" I cried in desperation.

I was tired, hungry and confused. I could not remember what we had done with the disk – perhaps we had put it back in the safe. I had better check.

I opened the door and was about to go into the corridor when I heard a noise. It sounded like a filing cabinet banging shut. Someone was in the basement!

"Oh, no!" I gasped. A burglar!

I ducked back inside the room and shut the door quietly. I put my ear to the door and listened intently but all I could hear was the pounding of my heart.

I waited a few minutes and then opened the door a little. I peeped out. No one was there. The burglar must have gone into one of the other rooms. I shut the door quietly. I was trembling with fear and not sure what to do. I could make a run for it, I thought desperately. I'd be upstairs with Sleepy in a few moments. Of course, Sleepy, no wonder she had barked so much when we came into the house.

I opened the door again and tiptoed along the corridor. A door ahead opened. I ducked into the nearest room and listened as the footsteps faded away down the corridor. I sighed in relief. As I moved back to the door I knocked my rucksack against some shelves. Something smashed loudly onto the floor. I held my breath, not daring to move.

The footsteps stopped. There was silence and then I heard them coming slowly towards me. My heart was beating so loudly it was almost deafening. I fumbled at the door handle, searching for a lock.

The footsteps stopped outside my door. The handle turned. I was trapped. I backed away from the door into the darkness of the room and tripped against a box.

The door opened slowly.

CHAPTER TWELVE

Quantum Mechanics

"Professor P!" I cried, staring at him standing in the doorway.

"Peter?" he said, surprised. "What on earth…?"

"Oh, Professor P," I said, standing up and rushing over to him. "You're back! I'm so glad to see you. I thought I'd never see you again."

"Peter, what…?"

"And the others, are they back safely too?" I asked breathlessly.

Professor P looked at me speechless, his mouth wide open in amazement. "Peter, what are you talking about? What others?"

"Tara and Sparky, of course," I replied.

"I'm sorry, Peter," he said, "but I haven't seen them."

"Didn't they find you?" I cried. "Didn't they come back with you?"

"No," he replied, puzzled. "Why should…?"

"Oh, well, at least you're here now," I said with a sigh. "Everything's going to be all right."

I paused to draw breath and then, suddenly feeling very puzzled, I added. "But how did you get back?"

"By car," he replied, looking at me curiously.

"By car?" I said, confused.

"Yes," he continued. "That's how I always go to Cambridge."

"Cambridge!" I cried. "Cambridge?"

"Yes, Peter," he said. "That's where I've been for the last few days."

I stared at him in utter disbelief. I didn't know what to say. Professor P had been in Cambridge! He hadn't gone back in time at all! I suddenly felt very weak. I slumped down against the workbench.

"What's the matter, Peter?" Professor P asked, rushing over to me. "Are you all right? You look very pale. Is that blood on your head? I think you've cut yourself."

I touched the cut gingerly. "I must have done it when I fell against that shelf," I said quietly.

"Let's go upstairs," Professor P said kindly. "We can get a plaster for that cut and have a hot drink. Then you can tell me what's been happening."

I followed Professor P out of the room and up the spiral staircase. Sleepy was waiting at the top and almost knocked him over with the force of her greeting.

Professor P took me to the bathroom and showed me where the first aid box was, then he went downstairs to make the tea. I cleaned my cut and put on the plaster. When I had finished I stared into the bathroom mirror. I had got everything completely wrong! Tara and I had broken into Professor P' safe, read his private notes, messed about with his experiments…

What was I going to tell Professor P? What would he say when he found out what we had done? Everything had gone so horribly wrong.

I opened the bathroom door and walked slowly down the stairs. I went into the kitchen. Professor P had made a pot of tea and put a large plate of biscuits on the table. He smiled at me warmly.

"Help yourself to biscuits, Peter," he said kindly.

I sat down and reached out eagerly for the biscuits. I was starving – I had not eaten all day!

"There," Professor P said gently as he poured the tea. "Now, what's been going on, Peter?"

I looked at him, took a deep breath and started to explain. "We came round on Thursday afternoon to build the metal detector," I said. "Floppy let us in. He was very worried, he said you were missing."

"Missing," he interrupted. "But I left a message with him to say I wouldn't be back from Cambridge until Saturday. Didn't you get the message?"

"No," I replied.

Professor P sighed, "Go on, Peter."

"Floppy thought you'd had an accident," I continued. "So we looked everywhere but couldn't find you. Then Floppy called us the next day when you still hadn't come back and we went into your diary room and opened the safe…"

"You opened the safe!" he said, raising his eyebrows.

"I'm very sorry, Professor P," I said quietly. "But Floppy was so sure it would help us to find you, and he was really, really worried. We found the disk in the safe and then we went to the cave to see if you were there, but you weren't, there was only the pyramid…"

"You found the pyramid?" he looked at me in surprise.

I nodded. "Floppy said it was a time machine and that you'd gone back in time and couldn't get home, but he could fix the time machine and we could rescue you so we loaded Floppy's new program…"

"Slow down, Peter," Professor P said. He leaned forward and a concerned look appeared on his face. "Did you say you loaded Floppy's new program?"

"Yes."

"Did it work?"

"Well," I replied, "Floppy was a bit strange at first, but then he seemed fine. He said he could get the time machine to work and when we went to the cave we thought he had fixed it, so we all got in the pyramid, but Sleepy ran off and I went after her, then there was a flash of light, and Tara and Sparky disappeared!"

"They disappeared?" he cried in alarm.

"Yes," I replied.

Professor P stared at me speechless, his mouth hanging open in shock, a look of horror on his face. I had never seen him like this before and it was terrifying.

"They are going to be all right, aren't they?" I asked anxiously.

"W...when," he spluttered.

"This morning, a few hours ago," I replied.

Professor P stood up abruptly. "We must go to the cave immediately."

He strode out of the house. Sleepy ran along after him. I tagged along behind them, exhausted and hardly able to keep up. When we arrived at the main cave Professor P crawled through the tunnel first. Sleepy and I followed him into the small cave. He knelt down by the computer attached to the time machine and examined it carefully.

"Will Tara and Sparky be all right, Professor P?" I asked nervously.

"I don't know," he replied grimly. "I just don't know."

Sleepy went up to Professor P and nuzzled him playfully.

"Not now, Sleepy," he said, gently pushing her away, "I need to concentrate. I must find out what Floppy has done."

Sleepy came over to me and lay down at my feet. I leaned against the cave wall and waited anxiously as Professor P scrolled through the pages of mathematics on the screen. After a few minutes I heard him chuckle.

"Everything all right, Professor P?" I asked.

"Floppy has increased the number of dimensions in String Theory to fifteen," he replied. "It's brilliant! Absolutely brilliant!"

I looked at him puzzled.

"Floppy's new program works!" he said in delight. "He's made a major breakthrough in theoretical physics. He solved all the M-theory equations and got the time machine to work!"

"So Tara and Sparky have been sent back in time?" I asked tentatively.

"Yes, Peter," Professor P replied, a serious look on his face. "I'm afraid they have."

"But why didn't the time machine go with them?"

"Not enough power," he replied. "The batteries are almost flat. Actually it's a good thing the pyramid didn't go with them – the tubes are so fragile they probably wouldn't have made the trip."

"Can we get them back?" I asked.

Professor P did not reply immediately. I looked at him with mounting anxiety, worried by his expression. Finally, he nodded and I sighed in relief.

"There is a way," he said, standing up quickly. "But we must hurry. We need to go back to my house as soon as possible and start work."

We made our way quickly out of the cave and onto the beach.

"What are we going to do?" I panted as I ran after him. Professor P was walking so quickly I could hardly keep up with him.

"We're going to build another time machine," he replied.

"Another one!" I said in surprise.

"Yes," he replied, "but a smaller one, in sections that we can easily dismantle – it will be a portable version. Then we'll return to the past in the old time machine, take the new one with us and when we've found Tara and Sparky we'll rebuild the new one and all return to the present."

"Will it be easy to build a small one?" I asked.

Professor P nodded, "I have everything we need back at the house. But we must hurry – the calibration of the time machine in the cave will be starting to drift. The longer we delay the more difficult it will be to find Tara and Sparky."

When we arrived at Professor P's house we immediately

went down to the basement and into a large storeroom. Professor P climbed up a metal stepladder and reached up to a high shelf. I steadied the ladder as he gathered bundles of plastic tubing.

"Can you take these, Peter?" he said, passing them down to me.

He stretched across to the left and grabbed at a large canister of yellow liquid.

"Careful, Professor P," I cried as the ladder wobbled.

He held onto the shelf to steady himself and then passed me the heavy canister. We went into the main workshop where he explained what we had to do.

"I'll make up the tubes in one metre sections," he said, picking up a tape measure. "So they'll be easy to carry. Can you help by filling them with the yellow solution?"

"OK," I replied.

"You'll need to wear these gloves," he said, getting a pair from the cupboard under the shelf. "The solution is rather corrosive."

I took the gloves and put them on. Professor P cut the first tube, sealed one end with a metal plug, and gave it to me. He watched carefully as I poured in the strong smelling fluid through a small funnel. I gave him back the filled tube and he sealed the other end. We started on the next tube and were soon making good progress.

"How does the time machine work?" I asked as we continued filling the tubes.

"Well, Peter," Professor P replied, pausing thoughtfully. "That's a very good question. Forget everything you know about Einstein's General Theory of Relativity, space-time curvature, wormholes and rotating black holes."

"OK," I said. That was easy, I didn't know anything about them anyway!

"Time travel is so simple. When you understand the real nature of the universe, nothing could be simpler. It took me

years of searching before I finally stumbled on the secret."
He paused dramatically.

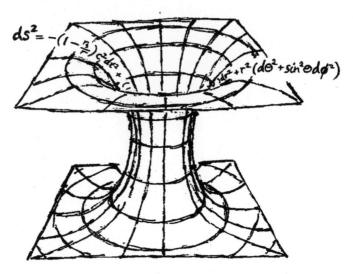

$$ds^2 = -\left(1 - \frac{n}{r}\right)c^2 dt^2 + \ldots + r^2(d\Theta^2 + \sin^2\Theta d\phi^2)$$

"The key to understanding time," he continued. "Is a theory that has mystified scientists for many years. Have you ever heard of Quantum Mechanics?"

"What mechanics?"

"Quantum Mechanics," he repeated. "I first heard about it at school from my science teacher, that's when I decided to go to university to study it. When I found out about Quantum Mechanics, I knew that nothing in my world would ever be the same."

I looked at Professor P in surprise. He had a childlike look of wonder and excitement on his face that I had never seen before.

"You see, at the core of science, at its very heart, is a mystery, a beautiful mystery. The way the world works is…," he paused, "magical!"

"Magical?" I exclaimed.

Professor P laughed. "Yes," he continued. "Quantum Mechanics was discovered by scientists experimenting on the tiny particles that make up atoms and they found some very strange things indeed. These 'particles' don't appear to be solid – they are spread out almost like clouds. Our whole 'solid' world is made up entirely of these non-solid clouds of energy!"

I was confused.

"I know it's difficult to understand," he smiled, looking at my puzzled expression. "Many great scientists have spent their lives investigating the meaning of Quantum Mechanics. Many of them don't agree with each other! But most of them accept that the foundations of science are built on a remarkable mystery. The mystery is this – our minds appear to create the 'solid' world that we see around us."

"How can that be?" I asked. "Are you saying that nothing is real, that everything we see around us – is just made up by our minds?"

"Yes, and no," he said with a twinkle in his eyes. "The world is real, but too strange for our minds to cope with."

"What's this got to do with the time machine?" I asked, puzzled.

"The past, the future, they're both happening now," Professor P replied. "Everything is happening now, every possible future, every possible past. But we don't see it. Our minds create an illusion for us, one we can cope with. Our minds are there to filter out everything except that thin slice we call the present. The time machine simply helps our mind to refocus on another point in time. It lets us tune into a different part of the whole. It's as simple as that."

It did not sound simple to me. How could everything be happening at once?

We continued working on the tubes in silence. I was stunned by what Professor P had said. If my mind was creating what I saw then… I looked at my hand, as though I was seeing it for the first time. If it wasn't real then… what was real?

"Good work, Peter," Professor P said when we had finished all the tubes. "Now we have to wait a short while for the fluid to set. I'll go and find a notebook computer and load the software onto it. I'll also get a few tools and some other things we'll need for the journey."

Professor P returned a few minutes later with two large rucksacks and a notebook computer. We wrapped the computer and the tubes safely in bubble wrap and packed them into one of the rucksacks. Professor P put the rucksack on his back and we went upstairs into the kitchen to collect some food and drink for the journey.

"Let's take some of my crisps," he chuckled. "I made them with my crisp making machine. I think you'll like them!"

We packed enough food and drink for a couple of days and then headed off for the caves. Sleepy trotted beside us wagging her tail as we made our way along the footpath towards the cliffs and down to the beach. I felt much better now and was looking forward to going back in time with Professor P.

We reached the caves and went inside. Once we were inside the small cave Professor P asked me to sit down in the time machine. Sleepy was a little unsure about getting inside but he gently persuaded her to sit on my lap.

Professor P knelt down outside the pyramid and opened the notebook computer. I waited excitedly in the semi-darkness as he typed away at the keyboard.

"All set," he said. "Are you ready, Peter?"

"Yes," I said confidently. "I'm ready."

"I've set the initialisation sequence for three minutes," he said, pressing a key. The tubes began to glow.

Professor P stepped into the pyramid and tried to sit

down. I moved to one side to make room for him.

"Careful, Peter," he warned. "You must be completely inside the pyramid. It's very dangerous if any part of you is outside."

"But there's not enough room!" I cried.

We tried as hard as we could but it was impossible for us all to squeeze inside. One tall professor, one very big dog and two large rucksacks would not fit into the small pyramid with me.

"You'll have to get out, Peter!" Professor P said as the tubes began to flash. "The time machine is about to start. I'll have to go on my own."

"No, Professor P!" I cried. "I don't want to be left here alone. What if anything goes wrong? I won't know what to do. Let me and Sleepy go first, then you come later."

Professor P looked at me intently for a moment and then nodded. "OK, Peter. You go first. I join you in a few minutes."

He stepped quickly out of the pyramid and the time machine sprang into life.

CHAPTER THIRTEEN

Prehistoric Island

A brilliant flash of yellow light filled the cave. I shut my eyes and winced in pain.

Sleepy barked loudly and the harsh sound echoed around the walls of the small cave. I opened my eyes and looked around. Everything outside the pyramid was fading away – the cave was hazy and Professor P a vague shadow. Then suddenly the cave completely disappeared! We fell downwards. Sleepy barked in terror and jumped up at me. I held onto her tightly with one hand and clutched desperately to the sides of the pyramid with the other.

It felt as though I was on an enormous roller coaster, plummeting from the highest point, down towards the bottom. But there was no bottom, there was just falling, endless falling. I felt sick and dizzy. I lost my grip on the side of the pyramid and expected to smash hard into the ground. It never happened. Instead I was floating weightless, like an astronaut in space. The cave had completely disappeared and outside there was only a dull grey mist.

Out of the darkness came a strong clear voice. "Prepare for secondary phase, expansion," the computer said.

The tubes began to flash on and off, slowly at first, and then more rapidly. I felt sick again and shut my eyes. The constant flashing lights had a very strange effect on me. It felt as though the light was inside my head, getting brighter and brighter all the time. It sparkled and flashed almost as if it were alive. Strange feelings began to overtake me. It felt as though my body was unreal, as though it were made of light and was dissolving into a sea of light.

What was happening? What was I seeing?

"Everything is happening now," Professor P had said, *"but our minds can't cope with it."*

"Everything," I repeated in a daze.

Was this happening to me now? Was I seeing all of space, the past, the future, everything, all at once here in the time machine? Were those stars and galaxies spinning and pulsing with energy, growing and then dying?

"Prepare for final stage, descent," the computer boomed.

The flashing stopped. I opened my eyes. A spiral tunnel of light appeared underneath the pyramid. We sped down towards it, spinning as we went. Colours flashed around me as we entered the tunnel, reds, oranges and yellows and then with a burst, a thousand tiny rainbows appeared.

We spun and tumbled our way through the tunnel. This felt far worse than before. My head hurt. I was totally disorientated as we raced through the tunnel, twisting and turning as we fell. Something must have gone wrong! We must be out of control! Surely this couldn't be right!

"Woof, woof," Sleepy barked frantically. I tried desperately to hold onto her as well as the side of the pyramid.

But the time machine was gone! It had just vanished, leaving Sleepy and me to fall unprotected through the rainbow tunnel. I yelled out in terror.

Then the journey changed pace again. It became smoother, less violent and as we floated gently downwards I sighed with relief and began to relax and enjoy this part of the ride. I spread my arms out and dived downwards through the rainbow of colours. It felt as though I was flying through a kaleidoscope. Sleepy wagged her tail excitedly and her ears flapped in the wind. This was fun!

The colours began to fade. The grey mist that I had seen at the start of the journey returned. Perhaps our voyage was nearing its end!

The mist began to clear. I felt a warm salty sea breeze blow across my face and could hear the sound of waves. When the mist cleared completely I saw the waves below me and I fell into the sea.

I belly-flopped into the water and, with an enormous splash, Sleepy landed beside me. I struggled to get upright and spat the salty water out of my mouth. I kicked and scraped my legs against the hard sea floor. I hardly noticed the scratch though – I was so relieved that the sea was not too deep. I stood up and the water came up to my waist.

Sleepy barked and looked at me completely bewildered, her big brown eyes saying, "Where am I? Why am I all wet?" I laughed at the look of astonishment on her face and patted her head.

I waded out of the water and sat down abruptly on the beach as my knees gave way. Sleepy barked and nuzzled her head against my leg.

"Don't worry, I'm all right, Sleepy," I said. "Are you?"

She barked confidently.

I looked around. There was no sand on the beach, only a flat rocky shelf covered with large boulders. The sea was crystal clear and everywhere I looked small emerald green islands sparkled in the blue green water. I had never seen anything quite so beautiful.

Was it true? I thought as I looked around me. Had the time machine really worked? Had I travelled back in time to the age of the dinosaurs? I felt a wave of excitement rush over me.

"Woof!" Sleepy barked questioningly.

"Yes, Professor P will be here soon," I said to her.

I glanced at my watch. Twelve o'clock. But it couldn't be – the sun was only just above the horizon. It must be early morning or late in the evening. I looked out to sea and noticed a slight mist hanging over the water. It was so hot! What would it be like in the heat of the day, I wondered?

I looked through the rucksack for some water to drink. After taking a few sips from the bottle I poured some into a plastic cup for Sleepy.

"Come on," I said when she had finished drinking, "let's get out of this heat."

We walked over to a small group of trees and found a shady place to wait. I sat down on a soft clump of ferns and lay back against a tree. The warm gentle breeze brushed against my face and I yawned. So much had happened and so fast. Sitting here on this tropical island I suddenly realised how tired I was.

"I think I'll just have a nap, Sleepy," I said, yawning again. "Wake me when Professor P arrives."

I lay down. Sleepy rested her head on my feet. Moments later I was asleep and having a deep dream. I dreamed of the journey through time, of spinning in space surrounded by flashing lights. Then suddenly I was plunged into deep water, unable to breath, gasping for air.

I woke with a start. Sleepy was licking my face. I sat up and rubbed my eyes. The sun was higher in the sky and it felt even hotter. I must have been asleep for a few hours.

I jumped up. "Come on, Sleepy, let's go back to the beach. Professor P should have arrived by now."

We went to the beach and looked around but there was no sign of him. I began to feel a little worried. Where was he? Maybe he had arrived while we were asleep and missed us in the trees. Perhaps he had gone to the other side of the island to look for us.

I climbed over some rocks at the end of the beach and walked towards a group of pine trees. The ground was covered in ferns and some small plants that I had never seen before. I bent down to look at one of them more closely. It had long thick leaves almost like a cactus but without the spikes. I touched one of the leaves. It felt strange and rubbery.

Sleepy ran towards the trees.

"Wait, Sleepy!" I cried. "Wait for me!"

She stopped and I ran over towards her as fast as I could, stumbling awkwardly through the dense ferns.

"Professor P? Are you there?" I called as we reached the trees.

"Woof, woof," Sleepy joined in.

I called again and listened. The wind rustled the leaves on the trees. A shiver ran down my spine. Was he here? Or were Sleepy and I all alone on this island?

We walked slowly through trees, calling as we went. We had only walked a few hundred metres when we emerged from the trees. Already we had reached the other side of the island. It was tiny! We couldn't possibly have missed him.

We carried on towards the beach and I sat down on a large rock overlooking the sea. Sleepy lay down beside me.

"He's not here, Sleepy," I said as I stroked her soft head.

So where was he? What had happened to him? I tried to calm down and think clearly. He must have set off just after us, so he should have arrived by now.

"Well, there's nothing we can do except wait," I said.

My stomach rumbled. I had not eaten breakfast and was now feeling very hungry. I rummaged through the rucksack and found a packet of crisps and an apple and some dog biscuits for Sleepy. I sat down on a large rock to eat. Sleepy nuzzled comfortingly against me as she chewed on her biscuit.

My stomach felt better after eating but I was beginning to feel lonely and very far from home. I was also feeling worried that Professor P had still not arrived. Maybe something had gone wrong with the time machine. He had said the calibration was drifting and that was why we had to hurry, in case we did not return to the same time and place that Tara and Sparky had gone to. There was no sign of them either, I thought. I gazed out to sea and wondered where they were. There were so many islands...

"Islands!" I cried suddenly. "That's it, Sleepy! Professor P must have arrived on one of the other islands. Tara and Sparky too."

"Woof," she barked, wagging her tail excitedly.

I rummaged through the rucksack for the pair of binoculars Professor P had packed and looked out towards the other islands. There were hundreds of them, all different sizes and shapes. Most were larger than the one we were on and all were covered with tall trees. I could see no sign of Professor P or Tara and Sparky but I did not have a very clear view from the beach. I needed to get up higher to see all the islands properly.

"Come on, Sleepy," I said, "let's go back to the trees."

We raced over to the centre of the island and found a tall tree. I climbed up it as quickly as I could and sat on a branch near the top. I had an excellent view in all directions. I put the binoculars to my eyes and scanned the islands again.

It was an amazing sight. I could see huge seal-like animals basking on the rocks by the nearest island. In the shallow water I caught a brief glimpse of a dark shape moving swiftly below the surface. I looked out towards the deeper water and saw a creature with a long slender neck and a round head. It rose up gracefully out of the water and then sank back beneath the waves. I felt a shiver of excitement run up my spine. So I really was back in the age of the dinosaurs!

Further out, I saw a group of large bird-like creatures flying through the air.

"Pterodactyls!" I cried excitedly.

One of them swooped down and skimmed over the surface of the water. I could see its huge skin-covered wings and long thin tail. It dipped its long beak into the water and effortlessly plucked out a large fish.

It seemed impossible that creatures so large could fly, yet they floated gracefully between the islands.

As I looked at the amazing scene before me I felt a growing sense of wonder and excitement. I was one of the first people to see these incredible creatures!

Sleepy barked impatiently from down below and I turned the binoculars onto the islands. I scanned each carefully, looking for any signs of life. Then finally I saw it! There, glistening in the sun, on one of the larger islands was the letter P, made out of rocks and stones.

"Yes!" I cried excitedly. "Sleepy, we're not alone!"

CHAPTER FOURTEEN

The Raft

This was fantastic news! I felt so relieved. I scrambled down out of the tree, almost falling in my haste.

"Professor P's over there, Sleepy!" I cried excitedly, pointing to the island.

She barked and ran towards the water.

"No, Sleepy! Come back!" I laughed. "We can't swim all the way over there!"

I looked out to the island. It was only a few kilometres away but without a boat it could have been a few hundred kilometres. I glanced down at Professor P's rucksack and wondered what was in it. Perhaps he had realised we might need to cross the sea and packed his solar-powered self-inflating dinghy. I opened the rucksack and looked inside. I found some bottles of water, packets of crisps, a sleeping bag and a metal box, but no dinghy. I decided to see what was in the metal box. I took it out and Sleepy sniffed it suspiciously.

"Welcome to Professor P's toolbox," it said suddenly. "How may I be of assistance?"

I chuckled. Trust Professor P to have a talkative toolbox!

"What tools do you have?" I asked.

"I have an electric penknife," it said proudly as the lid sprung open.

"Is that all?" I said disappointedly, peering into the box.

"Yes," it admitted. "But it's very good."

I took out a large bright red penknife. It had the words *Warning! Electric penknife* etched on the handle. I pressed the button on the side. The penknife vibrated so fast that I dropped it in surprise.

"Be careful with it," the toolbox added.

"Thanks!" I said, picking up the penknife again.

I held it firmly and switched it on again. The blade moved back and forth amazingly fast! I looked around the beach for something to try in on and found a large piece of driftwood. The penknife cut through it like butter!

I switched the penknife off, sat down on the beach and looked out to the island. Professor P had not packed the dingy, but perhaps I could use his penknife to make…

"Yes, of course!" I exclaimed. I could use it to hollow out a log and make a canoe. There was plenty of driftwood on the beach – I just needed to find a piece large enough.

"Come on, Sleepy," I called to her. "We need to find a really big log."

We ran along the beach looking for driftwood. Sleepy brought me a long stick in her mouth.

"No, Sleepy," I laughed. "Far too small!"

A few minutes later she ran over to a log, jumped onto it and barked loudly.

I went over to examine it. "Well done, Sleepy, but it's still too small, I'm afraid."

Half and hour later we had searched the whole island without success. None of the logs were large enough to make into a canoe.

"Well, so much for that idea," I sighed.

I looked in Professor P's rucksack again to see what else I could find. In one of the side compartments there was an aerosol can.

"I wonder what this is," I said to Sleepy as I took out the purple can. She growled when she saw it.

I examined the can more closely. It had the words *Superstuff* written in bright yellow letters on the side and *Environmentally Friendly, 100% Biodegradable* at the bottom. The can had three buttons on the top. I pressed the one labelled *Superstring* and a jet of yellow string shot out of the nozzle!

I chuckled. Professor P would never have packed anything as simple as a ball of string! I picked up the string and tested it. It was thin but incredibly strong.

"I know!" I cried excitedly. "We could use this string to tie the logs together and make a raft. Come on, Sleepy, let's get some wood!"

We spent the next hour working together, collecting driftwood along the beach.

"Well done, Sleepy," I said finally, collapsing exhausted. "That should be enough."

We had a drink of water and gazed at the large pile of wood in front of us. The four largest logs would make a perfect base. If I cut out some flat planks from the other logs and tied them on top of the base it would make a really good raft!

I began sawing the four largest logs into equal lengths of about two metres. I dovetailed them at the ends and tied them together to make a square base. When I had finished I tugged hard at the joins to make sure they were strong enough.

"Perfect," I said. "Now for the planks."

I chose a dozen of the straightest pieces of wood and cut them to the right length. I made notches near the ends so the string would not slip off and then tied them securely to the base.

When I had finished Sleepy jumped onto the raft and lay down, panting happily.

"Don't get too comfortable!" I laughed. "We need to make a paddle now."

I looked through the rest of the driftwood and found a long straight piece, which I quickly carved into the shape of an oar. Sleepy carried it to the raft in her mouth, her tail wagging proudly.

I tied the rucksacks tightly to the raft and checked that all the string was secure.

"Ready, Sleepy?" I said. "Let's get this raft afloat."

I took hold of one corner of the raft and pulled it towards the sea. It was so heavy that I could hardly lift it! Sleepy ran around, trying to help, as I dragged it along the beach. We reached the water's edge and I was about to push the raft out to sea when a wave came in. The raft lifted up slightly and then sank below the water.

"Oh, no!" I cried.

Sleepy cocked her head and looked at me as if to say, "Was it meant to do that?"

"Oh, Sleepy!" I said disappointedly. "Our raft sank. It's too heavy!"

We dragged the raft back onto the beach. All that hard work for nothing! I must have been stupid to think the raft would float. It needed something to buoy it up. But what? Then I remembered a raft race I had seen last summer – the rafts were kept afloat with blue plastic barrels strapped underneath them. But I didn't have any barrels.

"What are we going to do now?" I sighed despondently. I had run out of ideas.

As I sat staring at the raft I decided to look through the rucksack again in case I had missed something.

"Nothing!" I said in frustration. "Just this can of *Superstuff*."

Sleepy ran over to me and nuzzled me playfully. She nudged against the can of *Superstuff* in my hand and barked. I looked at the other two buttons on the can. One of them said *Superfoam*.

"*Superfoam*?" I said curiously. Foam is very light, I thought, maybe it will help our raft to float.

I held the can at arm's length and gently pressed the button. A pink liquid shot out of the nozzle and landed on the ground. It began to bubble and froth and make a curious hissing noise. I stepped back quickly. Sleepy ran behind me and looked at it through my legs.

In a few moments the pink foam had grown to the size of a football! I pushed a stick into it. It was quite soft at first but quickly began to set and in a few minutes it was so hard I could not pull the stick out. I lifted the ball up and found to my delight that it was as light as a feather.

"Perfect!" I cried excitedly.

I hurriedly took the rucksacks off the raft and, using a log as a lever, turned it over. I sprayed a thin layer of foam onto the planks and waited. The foam quickly started to bubble up. In a few moments it had spread out and filled the cracks between the planks. I waited for it to dry and then turned the raft right side up.

I dragged the raft back to the sea. Sleepy rushed over and together we gave it a hard push.

"Yes!" I cried excitedly as I watched the raft bob up and down on the waves. "We've done it! It floats!"

I grabbed the rucksacks and put them in the raft. I picked up the paddle and climbed on board.

"Jump on, Sleepy!" I called.

She ran into the water and clambered up onto the raft.

"Woof, woof," she barked happily.

I waited for a big wave to come in and pushed off hard from the beach. At last we were on our way to Professor P!

CHAPTER FIFTEEN

Shark Attack!

Once I was away from the shore the sea was quite calm and I began to paddle hard. Steering was not easy though! We went round in circles a few times before I worked out how to control the raft.

As I paddled gently towards Professor P's island I looked down into the crystal clear water. A shoal of brightly coloured fish glided past.

"Look, Sleepy," I said, pointing. "Look at those fish. And ammonites too! Real ammonites!"

She peered into the depths and then looked up at me puzzled. What were these strange creatures? They looked like large snails but had long tentacles that waved up and down in the water, gently propelling them back and forth.

The ammonites were fantastic. Hundreds of them, all sizes and shapes, floated gracefully in the calm blue sea. It was an incredible sight and I gazed at their brightly coloured shells as they sparkled in the sunlight.

It was such a beautiful day. The sky was clear and blue and a cooling breeze blew gently over my face. I stopped paddling and allowed the current to drift us slowly towards the island. I felt so happy and relaxed now. I leaned back against the rucksacks and enjoyed the peaceful journey.

A few moments later, a splash of water hit my face. I sat up in surprise. I looked around at the calm sea and wondered what had caused it. Then I saw a huge dolphin like creature swimming just beneath the surface. It jumped out of the water, its large eyes looking at me curiously. The creature seemed friendly enough; its long pointed mouth appeared to be smiling as it came over towards us. I recognised it instantly from the fossil I had seen in Mary's

shop. It was an ichthyosaurus.

Another appeared and then two little ones swam over.

"Oh, a whole family!" I cried in delight.

Sleepy looked at them and wagged her tail. She leaned over the side of the raft and before I could stop her, she jumped in.

"No, Sleepy!" I shouted.

But there was no need to worry. The ichthyosaurs were quite friendly and Sleepy had a great time playing in the water with them.

I noticed the current was pulling us a little off course so I began to paddle to steer us in the right direction again. The ichthyosaurs swam ahead, splashing happily in the waves but as we neared the island they swam off into deeper water. Sleepy climbed back onto the raft.

"Made some new friends then?" I laughed as she shook herself.

"Woof," she barked happily.

The current was becoming stronger now and I had to

paddle hard to keep us on course.

"Soon be there, Sleepy!" I panted, trying to keep us steady.

As I spoke the oar struck something solid.

"Oh, no! Rocks!" I cried.

I looked down into the water and froze in terror. There were no rocks beneath the raft. I was looking at an enormous shark! It stared up at me with cold menacing eyes. I gasped in horror. My heart began to pound. My hands shook with fear and I dropped the oar. I moved away from the side of the raft and looked around. I saw another shark, then another. We were surrounded. They circled us slowly. The largest shark knocked hard against the raft. I lost my balance and fell forwards onto my stomach. I lay still, unable to move as the sharks rammed again and again into the raft.

Sleepy growled. I knelt up onto all fours, trying desperately to steady myself. Sweat was pouring down my face. I was terrified. We were completely defenceless!

I felt a thud from the underneath of the raft. The sharks were below us, banging against the bottom. The raft tipped up and I grabbed hold of the side with one hand and the rucksack with the other.

Another shark rammed hard into the raft. I rolled against the rucksack. Maybe I could find something in it to scare the sharks away. I fumbled with the buckle and hurriedly opened it. I reached inside, desperately looking for anything I could use to defend us with. My hand closed on a smooth metal cylinder. I pulled it out quickly – but it was only a can of baked beans. I was about to put it back when I remembered this was no ordinary can of beans – it was one of Professor P's special self-heating ones!

I had an idea. I pressed the red button on the top of the can and counted, "one, two, three, four, five…" Dare I wait any longer? "Six, seven, eight, nine…" My hand was shaking as I counted, "ten." I knelt up quickly and threw the can at the closest shark. It hit the creature on the side of the head and sank slowly into the water.

There was a muffled bang and beans erupted into the sea. The sharks were surprised at the noise and two of the smaller ones swam away. The three large sharks remained. One of them turned and swam towards the raft, its eyes fixed on me with an angry glare. I reached for another can and pressed the button. "One, two, three, four," I waited longer this time, "ten, eleven, twelve", then, with a yell I threw the can as hard as I could.

Bang! There was an enormous explosion and hot beans burst onto the shark's head.

"Yes!" I cried as the shark thrashed its tail in surprise and swam off.

Now only two sharks remained. They looked at me suspiciously and circled the raft slowly. Suddenly one of them rammed into the raft, with its mouth wide open. A large piece of foam broke away and the raft dipped down sharply. Water slopped over the planks. I grabbed hold of a third can of beans. I had to get the timing just right this time. The shark turned and began to approach again.

I pressed the button and counted, watching the shark as it sped towards us. "Ten, eleven, twelve, thirteen," I had to wait for the right moment, "fourteen, fifteen", the shark was almost upon us, it opened its huge mouth. This was moment I had been waiting for. I hurled the can at the shark.

It landed in the shark's mouth and exploded. Blood and beans poured out into the sea. The creature thrashed around in confusion and swam off into the open sea.

Now, only the largest shark remained. It swam slowly and deliberately towards the raft. I reached into the rucksack for another can of beans. There wasn't one!

"No more cans!" I cried helplessly to Sleepy.

The huge shark drew closer and circled the raft, eyeing me cautiously. It swam underneath us and circled the raft again. I fumbled in the rucksack, desperately searching for something else. But I found nothing. I sank down in despair, holding Sleepy close to me. I had done all I could.

I looked up. The shark was streaking towards us, making its final assault on the damaged raft.

Suddenly the shark turned sharply away.

What was happening, I wondered? Why had the shark disappeared? It was then that I noticed a dark shape, a huge shadow, moving in on the shark. I held my breath. The shark sped through the water as fast as it could, fleeing the danger. But it was too late.

The sea exploded.

The raft was knocked backwards as the largest creature I had ever seen burst out of the depths with the shark writhing in its mouth. It was a monstrous animal, with rows of sharp teeth firmly clamped into the terrified shark.

As it fell back into the sea we were splashed with

seawater stained red with shark's blood. I held tightly onto the side of the raft as the wash buffeted against us.

I felt sick as I wiped the red seawater off my arm. I stared out at the sea in shock. What was that monster? Then I remembered the picture on the Internet – it was a liopleurodon, a shark eater. I had just seen the largest carnivore ever to live on earth!

I fell back against the rucksack. My legs turned to jelly and my whole body was shaking uncontrollably. We're still alive, we're still alive, I kept repeating to myself. That monster had saved our lifes.

"Woof," Sleepy barked and nuzzled forcefully against my arm.

I looked up and saw that we were drifting away from the island. I would have to row hard against the current to stop us from being swept out into the open sea.

"Oh, no!" I cried in horror. "The oar, it's gone!"

The oar was floating away from us about fifty metres in the distance. Sleepy dived into the water. I held my breath as she paddled frantically towards it. She reached the oar, grasped it in her mouth and began to swim back to the raft.

"Oh, well done, Sleepy!" I cried in relief.

When she was close enough I leaned over the side of the raft, grabbed the oar out of her mouth and helped her back on board. I thrust the oar into the water and paddled with all my strength. We had to get to the island as soon as possible, before we were attacked again. I rowed as fast as I could, not daring to look back at what might be behind us.

CHAPTER SIXTEEN

Reunited

As we neared the island I heard a voice calling my name, "Peter! Peter! Over here!"

"Tara! Sparky!" I cried when I saw them running along the beach, waving madly at us.

Sleepy barked loudly and dived into the water.

"It's great to see you again, Tara!" I said, jumping off the raft to greet her.

"Oh, Peter!" she said, giving me a hug. "It's so good to see you. But how on earth did you get here?"

Before I could reply Sparky barked excitedly and jumped up at me.

"Oh, Sparky!" I cried in delight as I knelt down and put my arms around him. "I missed you too."

"Woof! Woof," he barked. He licked my face and wagged his tail so hard I thought it would drop off!

"How did you get here, Peter?" Tara repeated. "And where did the raft come from. And what was all that noise and splashing and barking?"

"We were attacked," I said, dragging the raft onto the beach.

"Attacked!" Tara exclaimed with a horrified look on her face.

"Yes," I continued, "by sharks, lots of them, huge ones. And there was a enormous sea creature, bigger than a whale, it was incredible, it ate one of the sharks, just caught it whole in its mouth."

"Oh, Peter!" she gasped looking at me wide-eyed. "Are you all right? Weren't you hurt?"

"I'm OK," I said, collapsing wearily onto the beach. "Sleepy was wonderful," I added. "She was so brave. She went back into the water to fetch the paddle!"

"Oh, well done, Sleepy!" Tara said, giving her a hug too.

"Woof, woof," Sleepy barked in delight at her praise.

"Oh, I *am* glad you're safe now!" Tara added. "It's great to see you again!"

I smiled at her warmly. "Thanks," I said. "How about you, Tara, are you all right?"

"I've been really worried!" she said. "I didn't know what to do when we set off without you. I looked for Professor P but I couldn't find him anywhere."

I looked at Tara sheepishly. "That's because he wasn't here. He didn't go back in time. We got it wrong, Tara."

"What...?" she spluttered.

"He was in Cambridge," I added.

Tara looked at me, her mouth open in surprise. "Cambridge?" she repeated blankly.

"It was a mistake. Floppy got it all wrong."

"But..." she started.

"When you disappeared I went back to Professor P's house to get help," I explained. "He was there, Tara, he'd just got back from Cambridge. When I told him what had happened he was really worried about you. We came to find you and built another time machine so we could get home."

"Another time machine!" she exclaimed.

"Yes, a small one – it's in there," I said, pointing to the rucksack.

"But where's Professor P then?" Tara asked, puzzled. "Didn't he come with you?"

"He was going to," I explained, "but he couldn't fit in the time machine with me, the rucksacks and Sleepy. So we came first and he said he'd follow us. I waited for him but when he didn't come I thought he had probably arrived on one of the other islands. Then, when I saw the letter P on this island, I thought it was a sign from him."

"I made the sign," Tara explained, "hoping Professor P would see it."

"That was a good idea," I said. "I'm sure he'll see it and get here soon."

Tara nodded.

"What about you, Tara?" I asked. "What have you been doing? Have you been here long?"

"I got here in the middle of the night," she replied. "It was really scary in the dark and I felt very strange after the journey through time. Really shaken and confused."

"Me too," I said. "It's weird isn't it?"

"Yes, really weird," she agreed. "I was worried when we left without you. Then when I realised that the time machine hadn't come with us and we had no way of getting home, I panicked! But Floppy said not to worry, that everything would be all right."

"Where is Floppy?" I interrupted. "Is he OK?"

"He's back at camp, he's... well, you'll see," she said mysteriously. "Anyway when the sun came up I decided to explore the island and look for Professor P. I didn't find him, of course, but I did find a great place to make a camp. It's not far from here, in some trees by a dried-up stream. Come on, I'll show you."

We picked up the rucksacks and set off along the beach towards a group of tall pine trees.

"This island's really big," she said. "Just past the camp there's a large bay with huge animals lying on the rocks. I've never seen anything like them before. They're like massive seals with long necks – they're so heavy they can hardly move. And there are huge bird-like creatures on the cliffs. I don't know what they are, but they're enormous and look pretty mean."

"Pterodactyls," I said. "I saw some too. They're huge – I'm amazed they can fly!"

We arrived at the small dried-up stream. Tara and I pushed through the ferns towards the forest and Sleepy and Sparky jumped down into the old stream-bed.

"Here we are," she said as we reached a clearing in the woods.

"Wow!" I cried in amazement.

Tara had woven branches between the trees to make a large circular camp. She had put a fireplace in the centre and surrounded it with logs to sit on. Sparky ran over to the fireplace, stood on one of the logs and wagged his tail proudly, as if to say, "look what we've made!" Sleepy ran over to the little puppy and together they raced all round the camp excitedly.

Beyond the fireplace, over to the right, I noticed a shimmering hammock slung between two trees. I looked at Tara.

"Come and say hello," she said with a smile.

As we walked over to the hammock I saw a large owl

with a multi-coloured rabbit tail. The owl was lying in the rainbow-coloured hammock and was wearing large yellow sunglasses. He sipped what appeared to be a cocktail drink in a wide rimmed glass. It had cherries and a purple paper umbrella in it.

"Floppy?" I said tentatively.

"Hey, man," he replied, flicking his tail. "How you doing, Pete?"

"Pete!" I choked. Tara giggled.

"Are you all right, Floppy?" I asked.

He pushed the glasses down to the end of his nose and looked at me over the rims.

"Just chilling out, man," he added. "Thinking about things, you know."

I tried not to laugh.

"Catch you later then, Floppy," Tara said, starting to walk away. "Come on, Pete," she said. "Mustn't disturb the great mind while he's 'thinking', must we?"

As we walked away Floppy called out, "Hey, dudes, don't you want to know all the amazing stuff I've been thinking about?"

"Er…sure," I said, walking back to the hammock.

"I've just finished my Theory of Everything," he announced proudly as he sat up.

"Really?" I said, impressed.

"It's simple, but brilliant," he continued. "A child could understand it, yet only a genius could discover it. Professor P will be amazed, I can't wait to tell him."

"What is it then?" Tara asked curiously.

"It's the result of billions of complex calculations derived from Superstring Theory," he said seriously. "The solution is elegant and concise."

Floppy stood up, puffed up his chest and cleared his throat.

"In fact, it's absolutely perfect." he said pompously.

"Are you ready to hear it?"

"Yes," we replied.

Floppy took of his glasses and looked at us intensely. In a low voice, almost as if he were afraid of being overheard, he said, "I think therefore."

"What?" I said, confused.

"I think therefore," he repeated.

"That's it?" I asked. "Your Theory of Everything?"

"Yes," he replied proudly. "It is."

"Oh, Floppy," Tara giggled. "You're so funny!"

Floppy slumped back into the hammock crestfallen. "You don't like it," he said quietly.

"Oh, I'm sorry, Floppy," Tara said. "I didn't mean to laugh. It's just, I was expecting something a bit more..." she hesitated, searching for the right word.

"Mathematical?" I suggested.

He jumped up excitedly. "Mathematical? Of course, yes, let me explain it to you mathematically. Then you'll understand."

A black gown appeared about Floppy's shoulders and a pair of horn-rimmed glasses on his nose. A blackboard materialised next to him. He held a piece of white chalk in his wing and, at the top of the board, he wrote *The Theory of Everything*.

"You have learnt algebra at school, I assume?" he said, peering over his glasses.

"Yes," we replied.

"Good," he said, turning to the blackboard. "We start with the basic truth *I think therefore I am*. From this we can conclude *I think I am therefore I am.*

I scratched my head.

Floppy continued enthusiastically. "Now here's the brilliant bit. We simply subtract *I am* from both sides," he said, dramatically sweeping his wing across the blackboard and crossing off the *I am*s, "to give *I think therefore.*"

134

He paused and looked at us expectantly.

I tried not to laugh. "Your theory is very…"

"Interesting," Tara giggled.

"But perhaps it still needs some work," I added.

He looked at the blackboard thoughtfully, "Do you think so?" He paused. "Yes," he burst out excitedly. "You're right! I need to start with *I think I think therefore I think*. Then I can subtract *I think* from both sides. Or better still…"

Floppy scribbled on the blackboard and then stopped to scratch his head. He was all mixed up now, part owl, part rabbit and a few other animals I did not recognise.

"We'll leave you to it then, Floppy," I said, chuckling.

He noticed us leaving and changed back into the rainbow owl. The blackboard vanished in a puff of smoke.

"OK," he said, popping his large yellow glasses back on. "That's cool." He lay back in the hammock and began to sip his drink.

"Floppy's been acting a bit strange since we arrived," Tara whispered as we walked away. "I think the journey through time must have done something to his program."

"Professor P will sort him out when he gets here," I said, laughing.

We walked over to the other side of the camp.

"Look over here, Peter!" Tara said, pointing to a tall tree opposite us. "That's where I started to make a tree house."

"Cool!" I said and we both burst out laughing.

We ran over to the tree. A ladder was propped up against it.

"Great ladder," I said. I was really impressed. Tara had made the rungs out of sticks and bound them onto two long vines.

"I'll go first," Tara said as she stepped onto the first rung. "I don't know if it will take both our weights, so don't come up until I get to the top."

"OK," I said, eagerly waiting at the bottom.

A few moments later Tara yelled, "Peter, I'm up."

I climbed up the ladder, holding tightly onto the vines and being careful not to put too much weight onto the rungs. I reached the top and sat down on a large branch next to Tara.

"It's a great view up here," I said, looking out over the camp.

Tara nodded. "I thought it would be safer to sleep up here than on the ground. But I'm not sure we'll need a tree house now. I expect Professor P will be here soon and we can all go home."

"Let's finish it anyway," I said excitedly, "while we're waiting. It'll be great fun – I've always wanted to build a tree house!"

"Me too," Tara said happily. "I chose this tree because of the way these two branches come out so close together. I was going to lay branches across them to make a really strong base for the tree house."

"Good idea," I said enthusiastically.

"Yes, and look," she said, taking a notebook out of her pocket. "I drew some sketches of ideas I was going to try."

I looked at the notebook. Tara had done three small designs on the page. The first was a round tree house with a flat roof, like an African hut. The second was a tepee with long poles propped up in the centre. The third was an A-frame structure like a tent.

When I turned the page and saw her last drawing I burst out laughing. "If only!"

I cried.

She had drawn a split-level tree house with two storeys, a balcony, windows and even a tower on the top with a telescope and a flag!

"Well, maybe one day," Tara replied with a smile.

I turned back a page and pointed to the A-frame design. "I think this should be the easiest one for us to build."

Tara agreed. "I'm not sure how we're going to tie it all together," she said. "I used up all the string I had to make the ladder."

"No problem," I chuckled, "Professor P packed a can of *Superstring*!"

"*Superstring*?" she repeated.

"Yes, and there's an electric penknife. It's brilliant! I used it to make the raft. Come on, I'll show you."

We quickly climbed down out of the tree. I took Professor P's toolbox out of the rucksack and gave her the penknife.

"We'll be able to make a fantastic tree house with this!" Tara cried when she tried it. "It'll be the best tree house in the world!"

"The *only* tree house in the world!" I added happily.

CHAPTER SEVENTEEN

The Tree House

"Come on, Sparky!" I called. "Let's go and get some wood!"

The little dog barked and ran off into the forest with Sleepy chasing after him.

"Wait for us!" Tara cried.

As we pushed our way through the thick undergrowth I heard Sparky barking in the distance. We ran as fast as we could and soon came to a small clearing. Sparky and Sleepy were standing on an old fallen down tree.

"Well done!" Tara said, patting their heads. "You found a great tree. There's more than enough wood here for our tree house."

"Woof, woof!" Sparky barked proudly. He took hold of one of the branches in his mouth and tried to pull it towards the camp.

"No, Sparky!" I laughed. "We need to cut it up first."

He gave the branch another tug and looked up at us questioningly. Tara laughed at his expression.

"Do you want to try Professor P's electric penknife?" I asked Tara as I took it out of my pocket.

"OK," she replied eagerly.

I handed the penknife to her and she switched it on. She carefully started cutting one of the branches from the fallen tree.

"It's brilliant!" Tara said as the branch fell to the ground. She cut off more of the long branches and then we sawed them into smaller pieces. Half an hour later we had a large pile of planks, which we carried back to the camp and piled by the ladder. Tara climbed up into the tree and I passed the planks up to her.

"That's all of them," I said as she reached down for the last one. "I'm coming up now."

When I got to the top of the ladder Tara was already sitting on one of the branches holding the first plank in position.

"Have you got the string, Peter?" she asked.

"Yes," I said, taking the can of *Superstuff* out of my pocket. I pressed the *Superstring* button and a jet of the yellow thread shot out of the nozzle.

"That's enough, Peter!" Tara cried.

"I can't stop it!" I said. "The button's stuck!"

The string went everywhere. It burst out of the can in all directions and covered everything, including Tara and me, before finally fizzling out.

"Another of Professor P's great ideas!" Tara laughed as we untangled ourselves from the string and rolled it up into a big yellow ball.

Holding tightly to the ball of string, I edged out along one of the branches of the tree. Tara crawled along the other branch. I tied a plank to the branch I was on and then passed the string across to Tara.

"There!" she said proudly as she finished tying the knot. "That's the first floorboard done!"

We continued working along the branches, carefully tying down each plank. After an hour of working hard in the humid heat we stopped to have a rest and look at our work.

"Oh," Tara sighed disappointedly. "It's not very good. It won't be very comfortable sleeping on that!"

I stared at the large gaps between the floorboards and nodded in agreement.

"Maybe we could cover it with ferns," she suggested.

"It might help a bit," I said. "But it slopes so much, we'll probably roll off in the night!"

We sat down and had a drink. I felt exhausted after all

our hard work and unless we could even out the floor it was all a waste of time. There had to be a way…

"I've got an idea!" I exclaimed. "Let's use Professor P's *Superfoam*."

"What's that?" Tara asked.

"The stuff I used to make the raft float," I replied.

I picked up the can of Professor P's *Superstuff* again and shook it vigorously.

"I hope the button doesn't get stuck this time!" Tara laughed, dodging out of the way.

I pressed the button gently. "It's coming out OK," I said, relieved.

I sprayed a thin covering of the *Superfoam* onto the floorboards. The foam bubbled up and, while it was still soft, we spread it flat with a stick. A few moments later it was dry.

Tara knelt down and tapped the foam with her knuckles. "It's rock hard," she said, impressed. "A perfect floor. If we put a few ferns under our sleeping bags we'll be really comfortable."

We decided to take a break before starting on the sides of the tree house. It was the middle of the afternoon and we had still not had any lunch. I went down to the camp, returned with a few apples and sat on the foam platform with Tara. We dangled our legs over the edge and gazed out at the view. It was an amazing sight. I could hardly believe I was here, 150 millions of years in the past, in the Jurassic age!

"It feels as if we're on top of the world!" Tara said as we looked out at the sea, between the gaps in the trees.

"Yes," I nodded, "it's fantastic up here! I'm going to get the binoculars."

I scrambled down the ladder, took the binoculars out of my rucksack and hurriedly returned to the tree house.

"Can you see those pterodactyls?" Tara asked, pointing

to a group of dark shapes flying towards us.

"Yes," I replied, watching them glide past our island. "The big ones hardly move their wings at all – they just seem to float on the air."

I gave the binoculars to Tara and we took it in turns to look out at the amazing view over the sea.

"I wonder if Professor P has arrived yet?" I said as I scanned the islands. "I can't see any sign of him."

Just then, Floppy flew up to the tree house to join us. He looked out to sea through a huge pair of purple binoculars with silver stars on them.

"Hi, dudes," he said lazily. "Still no sign of Professor P?"

"No," I replied. "I don't understand why he's not here yet. He said he would join me in a few minutes."

"He'd probably forgotten about the Uncertainty Principle," Floppy replied casually.

"The what?"

"The Uncertainty Principle," he replied, peering at us over a pair of rainbow coloured horn-rimmed glasses. "It's a basic law of Quantum Mechanics. When applied to time travel it states that the more certain you are about where you'll arrive, the less certain you can be about the time you'll arrive. I've been thinking about adding the Uncertainty Principle to my Second Theory of Everything…"

"So when do you think Professor P will arrive?" Tara interrupted.

"Well, I can't be certain," Floppy replied. "That's the whole point of the Uncertainty Principle. In fact, that's exactly why it's called the…"

"Haven't you got any idea?" I asked. "A day, a week, a…"

"Well, if you want me to guess…" he hesitated. "Tomorrow. I expect he'll arrive tomorrow. Yes, that will give me time to finish my third Theory of Everything…"

"It'll give us time to finish our tree house too!" Tara added happily.

"Cool," Floppy said. "Let me know if you need any help with the colour scheme. It needs to be bright you know, bright and cheerful."

"Thanks, Floppy," Tara giggled. "We will."

He flew off and we burst out laughing. We climbed down from the tree and went back into the forest to gather more wood and ferns. We brought back some long poles and made two A-shaped frames, which we tied securely to the ends of the branches. Then we tied a long pole across the top of the A-frame and leaned some smaller ones against it.

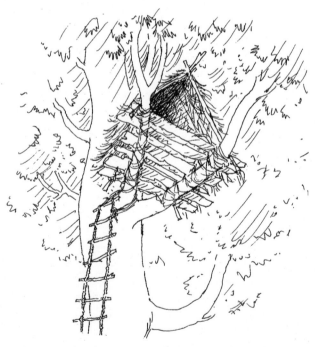

We used Professor P's *Super-superglue* to stick the side poles to the main frame. The glue came out of the can of *Superstuff* and it was bright blue! It was amazingly strong and set almost instantly.

"Floppy will love this," I joked as I sprayed on the glue. "Bright pink floor, yellow string and now brilliant blue glue!"

Tara laughed.

"What shall we do for the door?" I asked when we had finished tying some large palm leaves to the sides and back of the tree house.

"I know!" Tara said. "I've got just the thing!"

She dashed down the ladder and returned a few minutes later with a blanket.

"We can drape this over the entrance," she said.

At last we were finished. The tree house looked great!

"It will be getting dark soon," Tara said as we looked out at the sun setting over the sea. "Let's make a fire and have supper now."

"OK," I said, watching the sky change from pink to a beautiful red colour with streaks of purple.

We climbed down the ladder and started to make supper. I lit the fire while Tara unpacked her rucksack; she took out some plastic plates, cutlery, a loaf of bread, a can of spaghetti and a small saucepan. I found a can of dog food in Professor P's rucksack and gave it to Sparky and Sleepy.

Tara put the pan of spaghetti on the fire and when it was bubbling we put slices of bread on sticks and started to toast them. Floppy sat with us, pretending to toast his own piece of bread in the fire!

Orange flames suddenly leapt out of the fire. "Oh, no!" I cried as my slice of bread caught fire. I quickly pulled it out of the flames but it was too late, the toast was ruined and I had to start again with a fresh piece.

"Nice one, Pete!" Floppy said and his piece of toast burst into bright flames too!

At last we began to eat. "Mmm," I said as I took my first mouthful of spaghetti. "It tastes good, somehow different from at home."

"I think that's just the burnt bits!" Tara joked.

"Thinking about toast," Floppy suddenly piped up, "that's another important question for me to solve."

"What question?" I asked curiously.

"When you drop a piece of toast why does it always land butter side down? If only I could find the answer to that! It could be the key to my Fourth Theory of Everything!"

"Fourth theory…" I began but then stopped as I saw Tara shake her head and mime, "Don't ask!"

We ate the rest of the meal in silence, gazing into the flames of our camp fire. The dogs lay sleeping at our feet exhausted from the day's hard work. Floppy was perched on a log, his eyes half-closed.

"It doesn't seem real, does it?" Tara said quietly. "Being here on this island, millions of years from home."

"That's just what I was thinking," I said.

"And we're the only people on the whole earth," she continued with a sense of wonder in her voice.

As I sat gazing into the flames I tried to imagine what the rest of the prehistoric world was like. Eventually the fire died down and only the glowing embers remained.

"I'm pretty tired," I said finally. "It's been a long day. Shall we go up to the tree house now?"

"Good idea," Tara said, yawning.

Floppy opened his eyes. "'Night, dudes," he yawned.

"Are you coming up with us, Floppy?"

"No, I'll stay here and think," he replied. "I am still improving my Theories. By morning they should be perfect."

"OK," I said, smiling.

"'Night then, Floppy," Tara said and blew him a kiss.

I put out the fire and we were wrapped in darkness. The moon had not yet risen and the trees hid the stars. I knelt down and fumbled in my rucksack for a torch. I switched it on and we went over to the ladder leading up to the tree house.

Sparky and Sleepy lay down together at the bottom of the tree. Tara and I carefully climbed up the ladder. Once inside the tree house we sat on the floor and pulled our sleeping bags tightly around us.

"I'm glad you came," Tara said softly. "It was fun building the tree house together."

"It was great," I whispered. "'Night, Tara."

"'Night, Peter," she replied.

We snuggled down into our sleeping bags and I switched off the torch.

Within a few minutes, Tara was sleeping peacefully. I lay awake for a while, listening to the sounds from the forest and thinking about the day. I had travelled 150 million years through time, crossed the Jurassic sea in my raft, fought off prehistoric sea creatures... So much had happened!

As the wind gently rocked the tree house, I finally drifted off to sleep wondering what new adventures tomorrow would bring!

CHAPTER EIGHTEEN

Dinosaur!

"Aaagh!" I screamed.

I was surrounded by sharks! They were everywhere – coming towards me with their mouths open wide and teeth glinting. I hit out at them wildly with a stick.

"Peter! Peter!" Tara said, shaking me roughly.

"My raft's sinking!" I said, sitting up with a start.

"You were dreaming," she said.

"Wh…what?" I said, dazed.

"Dreaming," she repeated. "But from the noises you were making it sounded more like a nightmare! Are you all right?"

I rubbed my eyes and looked around. "Yes," I said slowly. "I think so."

Tara smiled.

"But it was a weird dream," I added, shaking my head. "I was on a raft made out of burnt toast! Surrounded by pink foam sharks! And I was fighting them off with a stick of spaghetti!"

Tara laughed. "Come on, Peter, let's go and have breakfast."

I poked my head out of the tree house. It was a lovely day and already very warm. The sky was a beautiful clear blue and a slight mist clung to the trees. I took a deep breath of the fresh air. I wanted this moment to last – the first morning on our prehistoric island!

"It's an amazing view," I said, looking out over the island.

Tara nodded. "Yes. So still and peaceful up here."

We climbed down from the tree house and were welcomed enthusiastically by Sparky and Sleepy. As we went over to the fireplace Floppy appeared and greeted us cheerfully. Tara and I lit the fire and fed the dogs. We sat down on the logs and had a bowl of cereal each.

"I wonder if Professor P's arrived yet," Tara said.

"Yes, I've been wondering about that too," I added. "I hope he'll be able to find us when he arrives. I think we should go exploring the island and look out for him."

"Good idea," Tara agreed, "let's put more P signs on the beach, with arrows pointing to our camp, in case he arrives on the other side of the island."

"Do you want to come too, Floppy," I asked, jumping up.

"Lead the way, man," he said lazily, a rainbow coloured safari hat appearing on his head.

I put Floppy's sphere in my pocket and we packed our rucksacks for the trip. I put a large bottle of water and some packets of Professor P's crisps into my rucksack. We put out the fire and left a note for Professor P telling him where we had gone.

"Come on, Sparky, Sleepy!" I called.

We set off. The dogs ran ahead, wagging their tails and barking. When we got to the beach we took off our shoes and socks and splashed through the clear water. Sparky and Sleepy chased each other in and out of the sea and Floppy joined in the fun – he turned himself into all sorts of strange multi-coloured flying creatures and scared the pterodactyls away.

After we had gone a few hundred metres we gathered some rocks and started to make a large letter P on the beach with a small arrow pointing towards the camp.

"That should be big enough," I said when we had finished. "Professor P will be able to see it from a long way off."

We continued walking along the beach. A few minutes later Tara bent down to pick up a small shell.

"Look, Peter," she said, showing it to me. "I think it's a piece of ammonite shell."

"It looks like it," I agreed.

"Wouldn't it be great if we could find a whole one?" she said enthusiastically. "We could take it home with us and show it to Mary!"

"Good idea," I nodded. "She'd be really pleased wouldn't she? Do you remember what she said, about how fossils always lose their colour? And how scientists would love to know what prehistoric creatures really looked like? If we bring a real ammonite shell back then they'll know for sure!"

"You're right, Peter!" Tara exclaimed happily. "Come on – let's see if we can find some good shells."

We searched the beach thoroughly but only found a few small broken pieces of shell.

"There don't seem to be any whole shells," Tara said, a little disappointedly.

"Maybe it's because there's no sand on the beach," I said. "The shells must get broken on the rocks."

We continued along the beach in the warm sunshine and soon arrived at a bay. Huge seal-like animals were lying on the rocks, basking in the hot sun. They had long graceful necks and four stout flippers.

"Look at the size of them!" Tara exclaimed.

The larger ones must have been over six metres long and they were so heavy I wondered how they could ever move! As if reading my mind, one of them slowly waddled towards the sea, dived in and then swam gracefully away, its long neck rising above the water.

"They look harmless enough," I said, "but I wouldn't like to get too close."

Sparky ran ahead confidently and went up to greet one of the smaller animals. It raised its head and let out a loud bellowing sound. Sparky barked in surprise and ran back towards us.

"Poor, Sparky!" I laughed, stroking him gently.

We skirted round the animals, going in towards the trees and pushing our way through the tall ferns. We finally reached the other side of the bay and were safely clear of the seal-like creatures. We walked back onto the beach and continued round the island. We stopped to make another P and an arrow and then sat down to relax in the shade of a tree and have a drink of water.

"This is the life," Tara said, lying back against the tree.

"Sure is," I agreed. "We should come on holiday here more often!"

After a short rest we continued looking for more ammonite shells. We had been walking for about half an hour without success and were tired from the heat when we arrived at a small lake. Sparky ran towards the water and jumped in. He disappeared below the surface.

"Sparky! Are you all right?" I cried.

He bobbed up again and swam around barking happily.

"He looks all right," Tara said, laughing, "and he's certainly found a good way to cool down! Let's go for a dip too."

"Good idea," I said, quickly taking off my T-shirt, shoes and socks. I ran towards the lake and jumped in. Tara and Sleepy ran in after me.

"Wait for me!" yelled Floppy. He disappeared and then reappeared in the lake, wearing a ridiculous stripy swimming costume and pretending to float on a lilo.

"I like the costume, Floppy!" Tara laughed.

"Thanks," he replied, touching his bathing hat. "I think it suits me."

We all had fun playing and splashing in the cool water and racing each other across the lake.

"Race you to the other side underwater!" I cried, diving under the surface.

When I reached the other side of the lake I noticed something shining at the bottom in the sand. I surfaced, took a gulp of air and then dived down again. It was a shell!

"Tara!" I cried excitedly as I burst out of the water, "look at this!"

She rushed over and I showed her the ammonite shell. It was the size of a small apple and the colours shone brilliantly in the bright sunlight.

"It's lovely!" Tara said as she turned it over in her hand.

We put it carefully on the bank to dry out and Floppy came over to look at it.

"Cool, man," he drawled.

A black diving suit appeared on him. "Let's see if we can find any more of them," he said in a muffled voice as he put on a pair of goggles and a snorkel.

We all began searching the lake. Sparky and Sleepy joined in too, barking excitedly when we found another shell. Half an hour later we had thoroughly searched all the lake and had collected five more small ammonite shells. We were about to give up when Floppy called out to us from the centre of the lake.

"What is it, Floppy?" I asked.

"Ammonite!" he yelled, "and I think it's a big one!"

We swam over to him as fast as we could.

"Look," he said, pointing down into the water with a red flashing neon arrow on his head.

There, almost completely buried beneath a large rock, I could see part of an ammonite shell.

"Well spotted, Floppy!" Tara cried.

I ducked down under the water and tried to remove the shell.

"Can't get to it!" I panted when I surfaced. "It's wedged in and I don't want to harm it."

"I'll see if I can pull the rock off," Tara said, "and you

try again."

We both took a deep breath and plunged down into the water. Tara heaved at the rock and lifted it just enough from me to remove the ammonite.

"Look at this!" I cried.

I held the large ammonite in the palm of my hands. It was undamaged and absolutely perfect.

"Oh, it's beautiful!" Tara cried. "Well found, Floppy."

"My pleasure," he said proudly.

"Mary won't believe it when we show her!" I said, giving it to Tara.

"She'll never believe where we found it either!" Tara added.

We carefully waded out of the lake and gently put the shell with the others to dry off in the sun. Then we sat down on the rocks and dangled our feet in the water.

"Do you want a packet of crisps, Tara?" I asked, reaching into my rucksack. "I brought some of Professor P's – he said he made them with his crisp making machine. There's every flavour you could want."

"And some you wouldn't!" she said, examining them. "Chocolate! Raspberry! Banana and custard!"

"He said they taste better than you'd think."

"Well, I think they'll taste disgusting!" she laughed.

We shared a packet of the chocolate flavour crisps and were pleasantly surprised by how good they were.

"I wonder where Professor P is," I said, opening a second packet.

"Do you think he got here OK?" Tara asked.

"I hope so," I answered. "He might be waiting for us

back at camp. I bet he'll be impressed when he sees our tree house!"

"Let's go and see," she said, standing up.

We carefully wrapped up the shells and packed them into the rucksack. We walked briskly along the beach, stopping occasionally to make signs for Professor P in case he had not yet arrived. Half way round the island we came to a group of large rocks blocking our way and were forced to go inland to pass them. We walked through the trees, chatting happily about our ammonite finds. Sleepy and Sparky ran on ahead.

Suddenly the dogs started to bark loudly.

"Sparky! Sleepy!" I called anxiously and ran over to them.

When I reached them I saw a half-eaten animal strewn over the ground.

"Yuck," Tara gasped, turning away.

The head of the animal had been ripped from the body and the carcass was torn to shreds. Blood and pieces of flesh littered the ground and the creature was almost unrecognisable.

"I think it's one of those seal-like animals," I said, feeling sick at the smell, "a baby one. And look, the blood's fresh, it's only just been killed."

Tara looked pale. "What could have done it?" she asked quietly.

"I don't know," I replied. "But I think we need to get away from here quick!"

We hurried through the woods, pushing our way through the tall ferns, scratching ourselves on the sharp branches, desperate to get away from the scene of death.

We were almost out of the woods and onto the beach when Tara stopped suddenly.

"Look, Peter!" she cried, pointing to the ground.

There were enormous footprints in the mud. Sleepy

sniffed at them and growled suspiciously. I bent down to examine the footprints more closely and noticed sharp claw marks on the ends of the toes.

"It looks like…" I said and then stopped.

"Dinosaur," Floppy whispered.

"Are you sure, Floppy?" Tara asked.

"Yes, there's no doubt," he said solemnly. I had never seen him so serious. "The claw marks are unmistakable. We must get back to camp now before it returns."

Tara and I ran out of the woods and onto the beach. I recognised where we were, it was the place I had landed in the raft. The camp was very close now.

Tara and Sleepy went on ahead while I hung back, waiting for Sparky to emerge from the woods.

"Sparky!" I called anxiously. "Come here!"

I ran back towards the woods, calling him repeatedly. Moments later he ran out, tail wagging excitedly. I breathed a sigh of relief.

"Stay close, Sparky," I said, stroking him.

As we set off to join the others I heard a rustling sound in the trees behind me. I turned quickly but saw nothing. I heard a branch snap then all went quiet. One of the trees swayed. I felt very uneasy and was sure we were being watched.

"Come on, Sparky, we've got to go," I said, pulling gently on his collar.

Suddenly Tara screamed. I looked round. Coming out of the trees was an enormous dinosaur. It must have been at least four metres tall. Its eyes were small and cold, like a snake's. Its teeth glistened in the sun and blood dripped from its mouth.

The dinosaur bounded onto the beach and I gasped when I saw its gigantic body. It came towards me so fast I had no time to think. I ran blindly towards the trees.

In my haste I tripped on a rock and fell to the ground.

The dinosaur turned towards me with its head lowered and stared at me with its teeth bared. I picked up a stone and threw it as hard as I could at the dinosaur's head but it bounced uselessly off its tough skin.

Sleepy came to my aid. She ran towards the huge creature, barking madly at it. It thrust its head towards her, roaring loudly. She rolled quickly to one side and backed away. Sparky joined in, barking and snarling at the monster. The dinosaur eyed the dogs suspiciously. It roared again and snapped its teeth at them. I could smell the stench of its foul breath.

Then a deafening roar filled the air. The dinosaur stopped its attack on the dogs and looked up. With a look of terror on its face, it turned and dashed into the forest.

"Peter!" Tara screamed.

I turned. Behind me towered another dinosaur. Meaner and much larger than the other, it stared straight at me and opened its mouth. I saw rows of huge sharp teeth.

I froze. The huge beast lowered its head and I looked in terror into the eyes of Tyrannosaurus Rex, the largest carnivore ever to have walked the earth.

CHAPTER NINETEEN

Leaving

There was nothing I could do. I lay on the ground and stared up at the huge dinosaur. I held my breath and waited for the fatal attack.

But the Tyrannosaurus did not attack. It spoke. "What do you think?" it said. "Not too over the top?"

I opened my mouth but nothing came out.

"Oh, I know what you're going to say," it continued. "You're going to point out that T-Rex didn't actually appear until the Cretaceous period, 50 million years from now."

Too shocked to move, I lay where I had fallen, totally confused.

"But you have to admit," the creature continued, "it did the job."

I cringed as the dinosaur moved closer. And then…No, it wasn't possible! The huge creature began to shrink in size! I stared up into its face, at its sharp teeth, its piercing yellow eyes, its long floppy ears, its…

"Floppy!" I cried suddenly. "Is that you?"

"At your service," he replied with a bow.

Tara came running over and cried out, "Floppy, well done, you saved us! You were fantastic!"

"Thanks," he said proudly and changed back into an owl. "I'm glad you liked my T-Rex impression."

I stood up and swayed forwards dizzily.

"Are you all right, Peter?" Tara asked, taking hold of my arm.

"I bumped my head when I hit the ground," I said, rubbing my forehead.

"That was a pretty mean dinosaur!" Tara said

breathlessly. "We're lucky to be alive. If it wasn't for Floppy…" She stopped and blew him a kiss. He blushed and looked away shyly. For once he was lost for words!

"Oh, and Sparky and Sleepy too," Tara added, patting the dogs on their heads, "you were so brave!"

"Woof, woof," they barked appreciatively.

"Come," Floppy urged, suddenly very serious. "We must hurry back to camp now. If that dinosaur returns I may not be able to fool it again so easily."

We walked quickly and quietly back to the camp. I looked around anxiously, noticing every branch swaying in the wind, wondering if a dinosaur was lurking in the bushes. I jumped at the sound of a twig snapping. Were we being followed? Was the dinosaur going to pounce again? Our island was no longer a peaceful tropical paradise.

"Any sign of Professor P?" I asked anxiously when we arrived at the camp.

We looked around quickly and checked in the tree house. Nothing had been disturbed; he had obviously not been to the camp. We went over to the fireplace and sat down on the logs.

"Oh, what can have happened to him?" Tara cried.

"He should be here by now," I said. "I'm worried, Tara. Suppose there's been an accident. Maybe he's been attacked…"

Tara looked horrified. "No!" she whispered.

I could not meet Tara's eyes – I looked down at the ground, feeling scared and helpless. Without Professor P we could not return home. We were trapped here. And we were running out of supplies.

"How much food and water have we got left, Tara?" I asked nervously.

Tara began searching through her bags. "There's enough food for a few days if we're careful," she replied, "but we're awfully low on water. I've only got one bottle left. How much have you got, Peter?"

I searched frantically through my rucksack with a mounting sense of panic.

"It's all gone!" I cried in dismay. "It's been so hot, and the dogs have been drinking such a lot! That one bottle will only be enough for a few hours in this heat."

"If Professor P doesn't arrive soon we'll..." Tara's voice tailed off.

If only there was fresh water on the island, I thought. I looked up at the clear blue sky. If only it would rain! But it was no use; we were on an island surrounded by water with not a drop to drink.

I looked down at the water bottle and suddenly felt very thirsty. Sleepy looked at me pleadingly, panting, her tongue hanging out. I poured a little water into her bowl and she and Sparky lapped it up eagerly. Tara had a drink and gave the bottle to me. I drank a few mouthfuls and looked at the bottle. It was already half empty.

Floppy flew down and sat beside us. "Peter, Tara," he said in a serious voice. "The time has come to act." He paused.

"What are you talking about, Floppy?" I asked.

"You have enough water left for only a few hours," he said. "Professor P has not arrived..."

"I know that, Floppy," I interrupted. "But what can we do?"

"We must start work immediately," he replied. "There is no time to lose."

"Start work?" I said, confused.

"We must start building the time machine," he continued. "It will take at least an hour to complete. We cannot wait any longer for Professor P. It would be useless to continue looking for him. We have no idea where he might be. We must return without him."

"Return without him!" Tara exclaimed.

"There is no choice, Tara," Floppy said in a grave tone. "We can wait no longer."

"But we can't leave Professor P!" I insisted.

"He may not be here," Floppy said quietly. "We don't know for certain what has happened to him. We must return in the time machine to find out and get help."

"But…" I began.

"Time is running out," Floppy said firmly. "You must follow my instructions exactly. Now start unpacking the tubes."

There was no point in arguing. Floppy was right. There was nothing else we could do. We had to start building the time machine and perhaps Professor P would arrive while we were making it.

Tara and I went over to the rucksack and took out the tubes. We laid them out on the ground and I counted them. There were sixteen altogether.

"Professor P cut them in half so we could fit them in the rucksack," I explained.

Floppy examined the tubes carefully.

"First you need to screw the pairs together," he said, "and then you can start making the pyramid."

We joined the pairs of tubes together to make eight longer ones. Floppy watched us as we worked.

"Now slide the metal brackets onto the ends of the tubes," he said. "Make sure they fit tightly. Next make the square base and fit the other tubes to each of the corners."

Remembering how the time machine looked in the cave we began to fit the tubes together to make the pyramid.

"We've done it!" I cried as we put the last tube into place.

"Well done," Floppy said. "Now you need to wire it up to the computer."

We opened the rucksack and took out the notebook computer and a collection of coloured wires and plugs.

"Plug the wires from the corner brackets into the connection box at the back of the computer," Floppy instructed us. "There should be sixteen altogether. Make sure they are in the right order. They should all be colour coded."

I plugged the blue lead into the blue socket. Tara plugged the red lead into the red socket. A few minutes later we had finished all sixteen wires. I switched on the computer and we peered anxiously at the screen, waiting for it to start up.

"What now, Floppy?" Tara asked.

"I need to set up the software," he replied.

"Professor P said he'd set everything up," I added. "He said it would return us to a few seconds after we had left."

"What did you say, Peter?" Floppy asked, looking at me intently.

"Professor P said it would return us to a few seconds after…" I began.

"That's it!" Floppy cried. "Oh, this is wonderful news!" He flew into the air squawking, his feathers shimmering with bright rainbow colours. "Wonderful, wonderful news!"

I looked at Tara puzzled, "Floppy…"

"Wonderful, fantastic, magnificent!" he cried, "Professor P is all right!"

"What do you mean, Floppy?" Tara asked.

"Don't you see," he continued excitedly. "We'll return a few seconds after you left. That means we'll get back before Professor P leaves."

Tara looked at me puzzled.

"Of course!" I yelled, jumping up in excitement. "Professor P won't need to come back in time to rescue us because we'll be safely home before he has a chance to leave."

"Yes, of course," Tara cried. "Oh, Floppy, I wish I could give you a hug! You're so clever!"

I sighed in relief. "Everything's going to be all right after all!"

"Come on, Peter. Let's pack our things so we can go!"

We dashed round the camp gathering our belongings and stuffing them quickly into our rucksacks. When the camp was cleared we climbed into the tree house to collect our sleeping bags.

"We made a great tree house, didn't we?" Tara said as we were leaving.

"We sure did," I replied, gazing out at the amazing view over our prehistoric island for one last time. "I wonder if we'll ever come back here."

"I hope so," she replied wistfully.

We climbed down the ladder and checked the camp one last time. When we had packed our things into the rucksacks we put them into the pyramid. I called to Sparky and Sleepy and we all settled into the time machine.

"Ready, Tara?" I asked.

"I suppose so," she replied, "but it all seems so sudden…" she hesitated. "If only I'd remembered to bring a camera! I would have liked to take some pictures of our island and our camp so we don't forget it."

"We'll never forget it, Tara," I said reassuringly.

I picked up the notebook computer and balanced it on my knee. Floppy flew onto the top of the pyramid.

"Click on the *Return Home* button when you're ready, Peter," he said.

I clicked the red button. The tubes started to glow faintly and the now familiar humming sound began. I held my breath in anticipation.

"Goodbye island!" Tara called out as the time machine sprang into life.

CHAPTER TWENTY

Home?

I shut my eyes and held on tightly as the time machine started with a blinding flash of light! When I opened my eyes I saw everything outside the pyramid dissolving into a grey mist. My stomach tensed as the ground suddenly disappeared and we plummeted downwards.

Tara looked pale. She clutched onto the side of the pyramid so tightly her knuckles were white. She opened her mouth to speak but no sound came out.

"Prepare for secondary phase, expansion," the computer said and the tubes began to flash rapidly.

I began to relax and enjoy the ride as the calming waves of light passed over us. But soon we were into the final stage of the journey. The wonderful feeling of lightness vanished. We tumbled downwards, twisting and turning awkwardly through the rainbow spiral. Tara leaned across and gripped tightly onto my arm. I clutched onto Sparky who whimpered and looked up at me anxiously.

Faster we fell, spinning, thrown around like a moth in a hurricane. We were completely out of control! The time machine was tearing itself apart! I could hold on no longer. Surely this was the end!

Then calm descended. We were floating in the grey mist again. I felt so relieved – the journey was almost over now. We would soon be home.

The mist began to clear. I looked around to see where we had arrived and gasped in horror. We were high in the air, hundreds of metres above the ground!

The mist completely disappeared and we fell downwards, speeding towards the cliffs. I clutched desperately to the pyramid as the wind blasted into my face. Seagulls scattered out of our way as we hurtled past them.

Tara screamed. I froze, too afraid to cry out, as I watched the cliffs race towards us. I shut my eyes and waited for the crash.

But the impact never came. For a split second everything stopped. We were suspended in mid-air, frozen in time, a few metres from the cliff face.

There was a flash of light. I dropped a short distance onto the beach below the cliffs and tumbled onto the sand. I couldn't believe it – I was alive. Somehow I had survived!

"Tara, are you all right?" I called out to her as I staggered unsteadily to my feet.

"Yes, I'm fine," she said, getting up and brushing the sand off her shorts. "What about you, Peter?"

"I…I think I'm OK," I replied, confused. "But how…I mean, did you…What on earth happened back there?"

"I don't know," she said, relieved. "But we made it! We're home at last!"

Sparky barked urgently. I turned and noticed Sleepy lying motionless on the beach a few metres away.

Sparky pawed at her still body and barked again. Tara and I rushed over to her and bent down to examine the big dog more closely. There was no sign of injury.

"Maybe the shock of the journey has knocked her out," Tara said, stroking her gently.

At Tara's touch, Sleepy opened her eyes and looked around in surprise.

"She's OK!" I cried as Sleepy got up and wagged her tail happily.

"What about Floppy?" Tara asked. "Where is he?"

"I don't know," I replied. "He disappeared at the start of the journey. I hope he's all right."

I took Floppy's sphere out of my pocket and tapped it twice. Floppy appeared as a grey fuzzy owl and flickered a few times.

"Are you all right, Floppy?" I asked.

"Wh…what, where," he stammered, "when…"

"We're home, Floppy!" Tara said. "We're safely home!"

"Wh…where's Professor P?" he asked, looking around.

"We haven't seen him yet," I replied.

"Haven't you been to the cave?"

"No, we've only just…"

"We must hurry!" Floppy interrupted. "We must get to Professor P before he sets off!"

Floppy flew off quickly towards the caves. "Come on!" he urged. "Run as fast as you can!"

Floppy's voice was urgent. We raced across the rocks as quickly as we could and arrived breathless at the caves.

"Professor P! Professor P!" Floppy called out as we went into the main cave.

"Sleepy!" I cried, pointing to the back of the cave. "Go find Professor P!"

Sleepy barked loudly and ran to the back of the cave. She dived into the tunnel with Sparky following quickly behind her. Floppy flew in with them. Tara and I climbed in last and hurried along the narrow tunnel as fast as we could. As I neared the small cave I was almost deafened by the sound of Sleepy's barking.

I tumbled out into the cave.

It was empty!

"We're too late!" I panted. "Professor P's left!"

"No!" Floppy cried, a look of horror on his face. "Professor P…"

Floppy stopped abruptly and flickered.

"Floppy!" I said. "What's the matter?"

"Very important…" he said and he gradually began to disappear. "Time machine has…"

"What?" I asked anxiously.

"Something terrible has happened…" his voice faded.

"Are you all right, Floppy?" I asked.

"No," he said, so quietly I could hardly hear him. "Low battery. Must find battery charge…"

He disappeared completely and we were plunged into darkness. Tara and I crawled back along the tunnel and into the main cave.

"Oh, this is terrible!" Tara said as we walked out of the cave onto the beach.

"We missed him!" I slumped down on the sand. I still felt sick and dizzy after the journey through time.

"Come on, Peter," Tara urged. "We've got to find Floppy's battery charger. Let's go to Professor P's house."

I nodded. Tara was right. We needed Floppy's help. He would know what to do. I rose unsteadily to my feet and we set off. As we walked back along the beach a reflection caught my eye and I looked up at the cliffs. I stopped abruptly.

"Tara!" I said, pointing. "Look up there!"

"The time machine!" she cried in astonishment. "How did it get there?"

I stared at the broken and twisted remains of the time machine. It was balanced precariously on a ledge, near the top of the cliff, at least thirty metres above the ground.

"I don't know," I replied slowly. "But if it's up there then how did we…"

"We should have been killed!" Tara exclaimed, turning to me with a look of horror on her face.

"Something weird happened," I said, shivering. "I can't remember properly…"

"Come on," Tara said. "Let's go to Professor P's."

We raced over the rocks and along the beach to the steps in the cliff. We climbed up the steps and sprinted along the footpath over the hills towards Professor P's house. When we arrived, Tara hurriedly opened the gate and we walked up the path to the front door. Sleepy hung back, sniffing at the gate. As we reached the door she ran over to us and barked.

"What's the matter, Sleepy?" I said. She barked again.

"She's worried about something," Tara said.

"Let us in, please," I said to the door.

The door was silent.

"Open up," Tara said. "It's us, Tara and Peter!"

The door remained closed.

"Maybe it's broken," I suggested. "Let's go round the back. We'll probably be able to get in through the kitchen door."

We walked round the side of the house and into the back garden.

"That's odd," Tara said, stopping suddenly. "The greenhouse – it's gone!"

I stared at the empty space in the garden where the greenhouse should have been.

"I don't remember that tree being there either," I added.

"This is really weird, Peter," she said, looking anxiously around.

I tried the door. It was locked.

"Peter, listen!" Tara whispered. "I think there's someone inside the house!"

167

Sleepy growled. I heard a door shut. Then the kitchen door opened and an old lady appeared in the doorway.

"Hello," she said, smiling. "Have you come about the garden?"

Tara and I stood and stared at her, our mouths wide open in astonishment. Who was she? What was she doing in Professor P's house?

"Wh...where's Professor P?" I stammered.

"Professor who?" she said, looking confused.

"Professor P," Tara burst out. "He lives here!"

The old lady shook her head. "I'm sorry, dears. You must have the wrong house."

I looked at Tara in disbelief.

"Maybe he lives in the village," the old lady said thoughtfully. "But I don't remember hearing that name before and I've lived here almost forty years. Why don't you ask at the post office?"

"Goodbye dears," the old lady said, shutting the door.

Sleepy barked and pawed at the door.

"What on earth is going on?" Tara asked. "What's happened to Professor P?"

I looked at Tara, speechless, too shocked to reply. We walked in silence to the front gate, both trying to make sense of what had just happened. Halfway down Farmyard lane Tara stopped and looked at me with a very serious expression.

"Something's gone wrong, Peter," she said slowly.

"I know," I replied quietly, hardly daring to speak. "But what? Where's Professor P? We can't have come to the wrong place."

"I know," Tara replied anxiously. "Everything looks just the same as when we left."

As we walked to the end of Farmyard Lane and down the main road I looked around carefully to see if anything was different. But no, the old wooden seat halfway down the hill was still there; so were the large house on the right and the broken signpost on the left.

"Nothing's changed," Tara said. "Except Professor P not being here."

"We must have come back to the right place!" I said. "But maybe it's the wrong time! Suppose we've come back too early, before Professor P moved into his house."

"Of course!" Tara exclaimed. "That would explain why the old lady had never heard of him."

"And why the time machine wasn't in the cave!" I added. "But how far back in time have we come?"

"It might be years!" Tara cried in horror "What if our estate hasn't been built yet? What if…"

We raced down the hill and turned into the estate. Everything looked exactly the same. We walked along the estate and stopped outside Tara's house.

"It looks just the same as when we left," I said.

"Let's just hope…" Tara said nervously. She took the key out of her rucksack. He hands were shaking as she tried to put it in the door.

"It doesn't work!" she cried, shocked.

"Try the bell," I suggested.

She reached out but, before she could press it, the door opened and Tara's mother stood in the entrance.

"Oh, it's you, Tara!" her mother cried. "I thought I heard someone trying to turn a key in the lock."

"Mum!" Tara cried, rushing inside to give her a hug.

"Is anything the matter dear?" her mother asked kindly.

"No, everything's fine," Tara replied. "Just something wrong with my key, that's all."

We went up to Tara's room and looked around. Everything was exactly as she had left it. Tara dropped off her rucksack and we hurried next door to my house. Sparky bounded excitedly up to the front door. I took out my key and put it in the lock. It turned easily. I opened the door and we went inside. I could hear the radio playing in the kitchen. We crossed the hallway and I opened the kitchen door.

"Hi, Peter, hello, Tara" my mother said as she closed the oven door. "I didn't expect you back so early."

We all went into the kitchen and Sparky trotted over to her.

"Hello, Sparky," she said, stroking him on the head.

Sleepy walked over to my mother, wagging her tail in a friendly way.

"Oh, hello," she said, slightly surprised. "I didn't know you had a dog, Tara."

"I don't," Tara replied, surprised. "She's not mine, she's…"

"She's Professor P's, mum," I reminded her.

"Professor who?" my mother asked.

"Professor P," I repeated.

"Is that someone you met recently, Peter?"

I looked at my mother in astonishment. Why didn't she remember Professor P?

We left my mother in the kitchen and went upstairs to my bedroom.

"This is getting really weird," I said to Tara as I shut the door firmly behind us. "Everything seems normal, but nobody remembers Professor P!"

"It doesn't make sense," Tara agreed. "Maybe Floppy can explain…"

"Of course," I cried. "He was trying to tell us something when his batteries ran out."

"We need a battery charger," Tara said, with a sense of urgency in her voice. "Have you got one, Peter?"

"Yes," I replied. "I've got one for my notebook computer."

I took Floppy's sphere out of my pocket and examined it closely. There was a small sliding door at the bottom. I opened it and looked at the socket.

"I think it's the same as the one on my computer," I said, picking up my charger. I plugged the charger into the socket and we waited.

A small red light began to flash. A few moments later Floppy appeared as a grey owl but much less fuzzy this time.

"Thank goodness you're back, Floppy!" Tara cried.

"Floppy, do you know what's going on?" I said quickly. "Professor P has…"

"Yes," he said in a very serious voice. "I know exactly what is going on!"

CHAPTER TWENTY ONE

Alternative Worlds

"What's happened, Floppy?" I asked.

"When we went back into the past," Floppy said slowly. "We changed it. And now we've returned to a different present from the one we left, an alternative world."

Tara and I stared at Floppy in astonishment.

"I realised what had happened," Floppy continued, "when we arrived on the beach and I saw you were wearing different clothes."

"Different clothes?" I said in surprise.

Tara gasped. "Floppy's right!" she cried. "You were wearing a red T-shirt when we set off, now it's…"

"White!" I said, dumbfounded.

Tara looked down at her own clothes. "But how…" she began.

"When we got back," Floppy said, "something very unfortunate happened that I was not expecting. The time machine 'flipped' us into an alternative world and you changed into your alternative selves."

We looked at Floppy blankly.

"This isn't the same world as the one you left," Floppy explained.

"Not the same world?" I said, puzzled.

"There's no time to explain," he continued quickly. "We must go and find Professor P immediately. He will know how to get us back to our own world. Let's go to his house now."

"We've already been there, Floppy," Tara said. "He wasn't in his house."

"An old lady was living there," I explained, "and she'd never heard of Professor P. In fact nobody's heard of him!"

Floppy said nothing.

"What is it? What's the matter, Floppy?" Tara asked.

"Professor P's gone?" he said finally, his voice shaking.

"Do you know what's happened to him, Floppy?" I asked.

"If Professor P wasn't there…" Floppy began. "He may not exist at all in this world. He may never have been born! And if Professor P isn't here we'll never be able to return home. Oh, this is all my fault. If only I hadn't…"

Floppy stopped, a look of panic on his face. I looked at Tara. Was Floppy right? Would we never see Professor P again? I felt a lump in my throat. I just could not imagine a world without Professor P, without his great sense of humour, his curiosity and his amazing inventions that made the world a fun and better place. But most of all because he was my friend.

"No," I said forcefully. "It can't be true. Professor P's got to be here somewhere."

Tara nodded. "He must be!" she said. "If Professor P isn't living here he's probably just living somewhere else."

"He may be," Floppy said, thoughtfully. "Perhaps we can find him. Do you have an Internet connection, Peter?"

"Yes," I said, going over to my computer.

"Try his old web address," Floppy suggested. "It's www.professorp.co.uk."

I typed in the address and the words *Page not found* appeared on the screen. I sighed disappointedly.

"Try searching for his name," Floppy said.

I hurriedly typed Professor P's name into a search engine and a page of results appeared.

"There is a Professor P!" I cried. "But it's a slightly different web address, www.professor-p.co.uk."

"Try it, Peter!" Floppy said excitedly.

I clicked on the link and a page appeared.

"What does it say?" he cried, flying around our heads,

desperately trying to see the screen.

"It says he works at Cambridge University," I said. "And there's a list of all the papers he's written on computing and quantum mechanics. It's got to be our Professor P."

"It must be!" Tara said, jumping up and down.

Floppy flew round the room in delight. "It is! It is!" he cried. "We've found him!"

"I'll see if there's a phone number," I said, scrolling through the screen.

"There's the number for his college," Tara said, pointing to the bottom of the page. "Let's try that."

I ran downstairs and returned with the phone. I could hardly dial the number – my hands were shaking so much.

"It's ringing," I said quietly.

A moment later the phone was answered.

"Oh, hello," I said. "Can I speak to Professor P, please?"

"Who shall I say is calling?" the college receptionist asked.

"Peter," I replied. "Peter Davidson."

"I'll put you through, Mr Davidson, please hold."

"They're putting me through," I whispered to Tara and Floppy. Floppy was hardly able to contain his excitement. He continued to fly around the room, squawking loudly like a parrot.

"Sssh, Floppy!" I cried. "I can't hear properly."

Finally the phone was answered.

"Good afternoon, this is Professor P's answer machine," a little voice squeaked importantly.

"Can I speak to Professor P, please?" I asked.

"No, he's extremely busy."

"Can you ask him to call me as soon as possible, please. It's really urgent."

"It's always urgent!" the little voice said, sounding

slightly annoyed.

"Well, this really is!" I insisted.

"Oh, all right, I'll ask him to call you," the voice sighed. "Give me your details, please."

I left my name and telephone number and put down the phone.

"That was Professor P's answer phone, all right!" I said with a smile. "Just as annoying as always!"

"Peter," Tara said, frowning. "What are we going to say when he calls back?"

"I…" I hesitated. "I suppose…"

"He won't know who we are," she continued. "And if we try to explain he'll probably think we're crazy."

"You're right, Tara," I sighed. "He'll never believe our story."

"He'll believe me," Floppy said. "Especially if I can talk to him in person and show him all my data files. Let's go and see him in Cambridge now!"

Floppy flew to the door. Sleepy barked and ran over to join him.

"Cambridge?" I said. "It's miles from here…"

"205 miles to be exact," Floppy said. "We can take the train to London and be in Cambridge by midnight…"

"By midnight!" Tara cried. "Our parents would never let us go! We can't head off to a strange city in the middle of the night."

"Oh, all right, we'll go tomorrow then," he said reluctantly.

Tara glanced at me uneasily. "What are we going to tell our parents, Peter? They're not going to be happy about us going to Cambridge by ourselves. And especially to visit someone they've never heard of."

I nodded in agreement.

"But we must go!" Floppy insisted.

"We could ask Mary to drive us," I suggested.

"Brilliant idea, Peter!" Tara cried. "Our parents will definitely let us go with her."

"If she's still here," Floppy added.

"What do you mean, Floppy?" I asked.

"Mary may not live here, in this alternative world either," he replied.

"Well, let's go and find out," Tara said, glancing at her watch. "It's nearly five thirty. Come on, we can get there before she shuts the shop."

Tara raced to the door.

"Let's show her the ammonite shells we found," I said, picking up my rucksack. "So she'll believe our story."

"Good idea," Tara agreed.

We left Sleepy and Sparky in my room and raced down the road to the village.

As we arrived at the bottom of the hill Tara stopped and cried out in astonishment. "Peter, over there! Look!" She pointed out to sea.

"An island!" I exclaimed. "That wasn't there before!"

I felt a shiver run up my spine as I gazed out at the island. We really were in a different world!

"I wonder what's on it," Tara said curiously.

"Dinosaurs?" I said with a smile. Tara laughed.

We turned into the village. Everything looked the same. I looked across the green and was relieved to see the Fossil Shop still there. We ran over to the shop and peered inside. The main part of the shop was empty but I could see a light in the back room. I raised my hand to knock on the door.

"What if it's not the same Mary?" I said, holding my hand in the air. "Suppose she doesn't know who we are, or…"

Tara knocked on the door. We waited anxiously and a few moments later Mary opened the door with a smile.

"Peter, Tara," she said. "How are you?"

We breathed a sigh of relief. "Really pleased to see you,

Mary," we replied.

"Sorry to disturb you so late," Tara added.

"That's all right," she replied. "Do come in."

"Have you got some fossils for me?" she asked as we went into the shop.

"Er...no, not quite," I said mysteriously, glancing over to Tara.

I opened the rucksack, took out the largest ammonite shell and gave it to Mary. She stared at the shell and then looked at us puzzled.

"It's beautiful," she said. "But it isn't a fossil."

"We know," Tara said. "It's a real ammonite shell."

"No, Tara," Mary said kindly, "ammonites are extinct, this must be some sort of tropical shell you've found."

She turned it round in her hands, held it up to the light and looked at the vivid colours.

"It isn't," Tara insisted. "It really is an ammonite shell."

"It certainly looks like an ammonite, Tara," Mary replied, "but they died out millions of years ago."

I unwrapped the other ammonite shells and gave them to her.

"Where did you get all these from?" she asked.

"We..." Tara stopped, not knowing quite what to say next.

"We went back in time," I blurted out.

"You've been back in time?" Mary repeated in amazement.

"Yes, in Professor P's time machine," I added.

"Who?" she asked, frowning.

"Professor P," Tara said. "He used to live here. We came to ask if you'd help us find him."

Mary shook her head. "Is this some kind of joke?"

"It's not a joke, Mary," I said earnestly. "We really need your help."

Mary looked at us intently. "Well, I've always known

you to be truthful. I think you'd better tell me what's been going on."

"Professor P invented a time machine," I said. "And we went back in time 150 million years."

"It was really amazing!" Tara added. "Really hot and sunny. There were lots of little islands everywhere. And there were pterodactyls flying in the sky."

"Just like in that fossil book you were reading the other day?" Mary said, smiling.

"Yes, but not quite, I mean…" I stopped, suddenly realising how unconvincing I sounded. "We saw things that weren't in the book too. Huge seal-like animals…"

"And a dinosaur," Tara added. "It attacked us!"

"But Floppy saved us," I said.

"Floppy?"

"He's a supercomputer," I replied. "Professor P made him. He turned into a T-Rex and scared the other dinosaur away."

"We're not making it up!" Tara said earnestly, seeing the look of disbelief on Mary's face.

I realised that Floppy's sphere was in my pocket. I put it on the counter and tapped it twice. Floppy appeared as a fat rabbit.

"Hello, Mary," he said and blinked.

Mary stared at the rabbit in amazement. She opened her mouth but no sound came out.

"What…" she finally stammered.

"Do your dinosaur trick, Floppy," I urged him.

Floppy turned into an enormous Tyrannosaurus Rex, so big he almost completely filled the room. He opened his huge mouth and I could see saliva dripping from rows of sharp teeth. He let out a roar.

Mary screamed in terror.

"All right, Floppy!" Tara shouted. "I think that will do!"

He shrank in size and with a pop he turned back into a rabbit but with sharp dinosaur teeth. He sat on the counter grinning proudly.

"I think I need to sit down," Mary said shakily. We went into the back room and she collapsed into an old leather armchair. "I think you'd better tell me absolutely everything, from the beginning."

"It all started…" I said. It seemed such a long time ago and so much had happened. Where should I begin? I looked questioningly at Tara.

"We were on the beach looking for fossils," Tara said. "When we found some gold."

"Gold?" Mary said in surprise.

"Yes," Tara nodded. "We broke open a stone and it had gold crystals inside. We looked for more but couldn't find any, so we decided to use a metal detector to help."

"Professor P said he'd help us make one," I explained, "But then he disappeared and…"

"Before you go any further," Mary interrupted. "Was the stone you found small and brown, with dimples on the outside?"

"Yes!" I replied in surprise. "But…how did you know?"

"I'm sorry to disappoint you," Mary said, "but a metal detector wouldn't have been any use. What you found wasn't real gold."

"Not real gold!" Tara exclaimed.

"I'm afraid not," Mary replied. "It's a type of iron ore, iron pyrites to be exact. It's often called fool's gold because it looks so much like real gold. It's quite common on the beach around here."

"Oh," we said disappointedly.

"I'm sorry to have interrupted you," Mary said kindly. "Please go on with your story."

"We went to Professor P's house to build the metal detector," Tara continued, "but he wasn't there. We looked everywhere for him and Floppy was really worried."

"Then we found the pyramid in the cave," I added, "and Floppy said it was a time machine! He said Professor P had gone back in time and we had to rescue him or he'd be lost forever."

"I'm very sorry about that," Floppy said apologetically.

Mary listened patiently as we told her how we had gone back in time to the Jurassic Period. She was fascinated to hear about the prehistoric island and asked us to describe all the creatures we had seen.

"What an incredible adventure you've been on!" she said, glancing down at the ammonite shells in her lap. "I would have loved to have been there with you. And when did you get home?"

"We're not home!" I replied. "That's why we came to see you – to ask you to help us."

"Not home?" she said, puzzled.

"We've come back to the wrong world," I explained. "It's not the same as the one we left. In our world Professor P lived here by the sea and was an amazing inventor. But in this world he lives in Cambridge."

"We need to go and see Professor P," Tara said, "and tell him what has happened so he can get us back into the world we left."

"Please can you take us to see him, Mary?" I asked.

Mary looked at us thoughtfully and then smiled.

"Of course I'll take you!" she replied.

CHAPTER TWENTY TWO

Cambridge

We decided to go to Cambridge early the next day. When Tara came round I was waiting for her in the living room with Sleepy and Sparky.

"Hi, Tara," I said as she came into the hallway.

"Hi, Peter," she replied, smiling. "All ready?"

I nodded.

A few minutes later, at exactly seven o'clock, a car pulled up outside my house.

"That'll be Mary!" I cried excitedly and we all rushed out to meet her.

Mary was sitting in a very old car, light green in colour with wooden panels, and in spotless condition. She opened the doors and Sleepy leapt onto the back seat. I climbed into the back with Sparky, and Tara sat in the front.

"This is a great car," Tara said as we set off.

"Thanks," Mary replied proudly. "She's a Morris Minor – over fifty years old and still going strong!"

The old car chugged up the hill out of the village and down the lane to the main road. As we drove through the beautiful Dorset countryside we talked happily about our trip to Cambridge.

"I went on the internet last night," I said, "and printed out some tourist information and maps of Cambridge."

"That was a good idea, Peter. What did you discover?" Mary asked.

I took the printouts out of my bag. "It says that the famous University City of Cambridge is noted for its historic colleges, the first founded in 1284. It also says sixty-three Nobel prize-winners are linked with Cambridge."

"I wonder if Professor P is one of them," Tara said.

"I'm looking forward to meeting him," Mary added cheerfully.

"You'll really like him," I said enthusiastically. "He's made the most amazing inventions! And they all talk! His toaster tells jokes, his answer machine sings, but his fridge is always grumpy!"

Mary laughed.

"I wonder if he'll be any different," Tara said thoughtfully. "I mean, in this world he works at a University, maybe he's not an inventor at all."

"True," I nodded. "I don't know what he'll say when we tell him our story."

"Well, I don't think I would have believed you if it hadn't been for Floppy and his dinosaur impression!" Mary remarked.

I realised that Floppy had been unusually quiet during the journey and I wondered if he was all right. I put my hand into my pocket to take out his sphere.

"Oh, no!" I cried. "I put Floppy on charge last night and I've forgotten to bring him with us!"

"What!" Tara exclaimed. "We've got to have Floppy! Professor P won't believe us without him. We've got to turn back and get him!"

"I'm sorry, Tara!" Mary said. "We're on the motorway now and it would take too long to turn back – I'm afraid we wouldn't be able to make it to Cambridge and back in a day. I'm sure we'll be able to convince Professor P of your story without Floppy."

Tara turned round and looked at me anxiously.

"Sorry, Tara," I said quietly.

I felt annoyed with myself for forgetting Floppy and worried that Professor P would not believe us without him. As we drove along the motorway I tried to rehearse in my mind what we could say to Professor P to convince him our story was true. But all I could imagine was a very awkward and embarrassing scene.

After an hour and a half on the motorway we stopped for a short break at a service station. Tara and I changed places when we set off again and an hour later we came to the Cambridge exit.

"Peter, do you think you could look at your maps and give me directions to the college?" Mary asked as we left the motorway. "We're quite close to the centre now."

"I'll try," I said, leafing through the printouts.

I found the map of the city centre and Tara and I tried to work out exactly where we were.

"Have we gone over the river yet, Mary?" I asked.

"We're just coming to a bridge…" Mary replied, glancing out of the side window. "Yes, we're crossing the river now."

"I think we're here, in Silver Street," I said, pointing to the map. Tara leaned over to have a look.

"Which way now?" Mary asked, seeing the road ahead curve sharply round to the right.

"Left!" Tara and I shouted together.

"Hold on!" Mary said as she spun the steering wheel and we screeched round the corner, narrowly missing a bicycle.

"Oh, I don't think we should be driving down here," she said nervously as the car hit a cobbled stretch of road and a crowd of tourists scattered out of the way. "I think it's only for pedestrians!"

As we drove down the cobbled street Sleepy put her head out of the window and wagged her tail. She began to bark loudly at the sight of an old building on our right.

"Stop, Mary!" Tara cried suddenly. "That's it! Professor P's college! I recognise it from the pictures."

Mary stopped the car in front of the college.

"I can't park here," she said, rather flustered. "You'll have to get out and wait for me while I find a car park."

"OK," I said, quickly getting out of the car.

Sleepy and Sparky jumped out and ran towards the college entrance. It was an imposing stone building, with wide steps leading up to a high wooden archway.

"Wait for us!" I cried out to the dogs as they bounded up the steps.

They waited at the top of the steps, wagging their tails and sniffing at the ground excitedly. Tara and I climbed up the steps and walked through the archway into a courtyard with a large square lawn surrounded by high stone buildings. Underneath the windows of the buildings were boxes filled with flowers and in the far-left corner was a small church with a colourful stained-glass window.

"It's really pretty," Tara said, looking around the courtyard.

Sleepy could no longer contain her excitement. She ran across the grass towards an archway in the far-left corner of the courtyard. Sparky ran after her, barking loudly. A man in a dark suit rushed out of a small office inside the archway.

"What are those dogs doing here?" he shouted. "No dogs allowed in the college!"

"Sorry," I said quietly as I looked at the disapproving expression on his face.

We ran over to the dogs and put them on their leads. We left the college and waited for Mary in the street by the entrance. Twenty minutes later she finally arrived.

"It took ages to park," she explained breathlessly. "I got stuck in the one way system."

I tied the dogs up outside the college entrance and Mary, Tara and I went back up the steps and into the college.

"We'd better go to the porter's lodge," Mary said, "and find out how to get to Professor P's room."

We went into the small office inside the archway and Mary spoke to the man in the black suit.

"Can you help us?" she said. "We're looking for Professor P."

"Is he expecting you?"

"Er, not quite," she replied, smiling at us.

The porter picked up the phone and dialled through to his room.

"Just his stupid answering machine!" he growled as he put down the phone. "You'd better try his room, it's number P1."

We stepped out of the porter's lodge and he gave us directions.

"See that archway over there on the left," he said, pointing across the courtyard. "Go through there to the old court. Directly opposite you is P staircase. His room is on the first floor."

We walked around the lawn to the archway and through

it into a smaller round courtyard. I stopped and nervously looked up at the old buildings.

"It'll be OK," Mary said reassuringly. "I'm sure Professor P will be happy to see us. Come on."

We walked around the courtyard to P staircase, climbed up a flight of stairs and stopped outside a large wooden door with the words *Professor P's Place* written above it. Tara looked at me anxiously. Mary knocked on the door.

"Come in," a voice called out.

CHAPTER TWENTY THREE

Professor P?

Mary opened the door and we stepped into the room. It was a large cluttered room with a stone fireplace and a piano in the far corner. The walls were lined with shelves bursting with books. Papers were scattered all over the floor. A man in a grey suit and dark blue tie was sitting in an armchair drinking a cup of tea.

"Hello," Mary said, "are you Professor P?"

"Yes, I am," he said, getting up out of his chair. "Can I help you?"

I looked at Tara horrified! This was not the Professor P we knew. He had the same dark hair, the same greyish beard, the same voice – but he looked so different in his drab suit. The sparkle in his eyes had gone and he had a very unhappy expression on his face.

"My name is Mary," she said. "I'd like you to meet my friends Peter and Tara. We'd like to talk to you about..." she paused, not knowing quite what to say. "It's difficult to explain," she continued, glancing at Tara and me.

"Please take a seat," Professor P said politely.

"Thank you," Mary said and we sat down on the large sofa. "We live in a village on the Dorset coast and we drove here today to talk to you about something very important."

She hesitated again, not sure how to continue. I was lost for words and didn't know quite what to say either. There was an awkward silence.

"How are you, Professor P?" Tara suddenly blurted out. "It's good to see you again."

"I'm fine," he said, slightly confused. "But have we met before?"

"Oh, yes," Tara replied.

"Well, I'm afraid I don't recognise you," Professor P said thoughtfully. "I don't have a very good memory for faces. When did we meet?"

"Oh, *you've* never met us," I began. "But we know you really well."

He now looked extremely puzzled.

"You know me but I don't know you," he said, shaking his head. "How can that be?" He paused. "Perhaps you've read my latest book?" he suggested. "Although I didn't think *Irreversibility in Quantum Computing* was very suitable for children."

"No, we haven't read any of your books," we replied.

"Oh, well, maybe you heard me on the radio recently?"

We shook our heads.

"You've been to one of my lectures!" he said in surprise.

"No," I replied.

"Well, how do you know me then?" he asked, scratching his chin.

"You, er…" I hesitated. "You used to live near us in a cottage…"

"By the sea," Tara added.

"I did?" he said, perplexed.

"You were an inventor," I continued. "You invented all sorts of amazing things. And your house was full of talking gadgets. The toaster told jokes!"

"Jokes!" he exclaimed.

"Yes," I said, "and you even invented chocolate flavour crisps…"

Professor P smiled. "It sounds as though you do know me – I've always wanted to be an inventor and live by the sea! Maybe when I retire," he added, gazing wistfully out of the window.

"You also invented a supercomputer called Floppy…" I

continued.

"He looks like a rabbit," Tara added. "Or sometimes like an owl, but I'm afraid we forgot to bring him with us."

Professor P looked at us and frowned. He didn't believe us! I had a sinking feeling in my stomach. I looked at Tara in dismay.

"You also made a time machine," I said quickly.

"A time machine?" he repeated blankly.

"Yes," I replied, "and we thought you'd gone back in time. So we went to find you…"

"But you hadn't!" Tara interrupted, "and when we got back home you weren't there, you were here."

Professor P looked at us silently.

"I know it sounds a bit unbelievable," I said nervously.

"It does," he agreed. "Highly unbelievable. And you've come all the way here to tell me this?"

We nodded.

He looked at us intently and then spoke again. "Well, I can't think of any reason why you would invent such an amazing story. You'd better tell me more."

I breathed a sigh of relief and we told Professor P everything. He listened patiently with his hands folded neatly in his lap as we explained how we had gone back in time to the prehistoric island. He chuckled merrily when we told him how we used his *Superstuff* to make our tree house and he showed great interest when we explained how we had assembled the time machine with Floppy's help and returned to the present.

"Can you describe what the time machine looked like?" he asked eagerly.

"It was a pyramid about this high," I replied, showing him with my hands, "made of plastic tubes filled with yellow liquid. And it had wires connecting it to a notebook computer."

"I see," he said, nodding, "please continue."

"When we arrived back at your house there was an old lady living there. Sleepy kept barking and…"

"Sleepy? Did you say Sleepy?" he said, jumping up out of his chair.

"Yes," I replied, surprised by his reaction. "She's your dog."

"I… I had a dog called Sleepy," he said, his voice shaking with emotion. "But she died earlier this year. She was run over by a car."

"No, Professor P," Tara said firmly. "She's alive."

He looked at us in disbelief.

"We brought her with us," I added.

"You've brought her here?" he repeated.

"Yes," I replied. "We tied her up outside the main gate because the man in the office said we couldn't bring her…"

Before I could finish my sentence Professor P raced out of the door, flew down the stairs and ran across the Old Court. We followed him as fast as we could.

When Sleepy saw Professor P she broke loose from her lead and bounded towards him. They met in the centre of the courtyard. She jumped up at him with so much excitement that he was knocked to the ground!

"Oh, Sleepy!" he spluttered as she sat on his chest and licked the tears rolling down his cheeks.

"Woof, woof!" she barked madly, desperately excited to see him again.

When Professor P finally managed to sit up Sleepy ran around him in circles, wagging her tail vigorously.

"Oh, Sleepy, it really is you!" Professor P said as he stroked her head. "I've missed you so much. I thought I'd lost you forever!"

Mary beckoned to us, "I think we should leave Professor P and Sleepy together for a while," she whispered. "Let's wait for them by the entrance."

We went over to the gate, I untied Sparky and we waited quietly for Professor P and Sleepy. When they came over to us Professor P was grinning from ear to ear. He had taken off his jacket, his tie was loose and that old familiar sparkle was back in his eyes.

"Thank you," he said softly, "I cannot thank you enough for bringing Sleepy back to me! This calls for a celebration! Let me take you to lunch, you must be hungry after your long journey."

I nodded. I was starving!

"There's a lovely little tea room not far away, just off King's Parade," he continued. "Let's go there."

We set off down the street towards the teashop. Professor P strode along happily with a smile on his face, a spring in his step and Sleepy at his heels. When we arrived at the teashop we sat at a table outside in the sun, opposite an old church. Sleepy lay contentedly at Professor P's feet and Sparky at mine.

"So," Professor P said, looking at Tara and me curiously. "Alternative worlds really do exist!"

"Can you explain what's happened, Professor P?" Mary asked. "In simple terms!"

"I'm not sure I fully understand it all myself," he replied, glancing down at Sleepy. "This is an astounding scientific discovery. If alternative worlds are real..." he paused, "then other universes exist and all things are possible!"

He was silent for a moment, a look of intense concentration on his face and then he turned to us and said, "Do please go on with your story. You didn't quite finish with all the excitement over Sleepy."

"When you weren't at your house," I continued, "Tara and I went home and plugged Floppy into my battery charger. He told us that the time machine had gone wrong and we had returned to an alternative world."

"He said we had to find you, Professor P," Tara added, "so you could fix the time machine and get us home, back to our own world."

"I see," Professor P said thoughtfully. "I'm afraid that may not be very easy. In this world I'm a university lecturer, not an inventor, and I know very little about time machines. In fact," he paused and looked at us awkwardly. "I'm not sure I can help you at all."

"But we've got to get back!" I cried, horrified.

"Why?" Professor P asked, taken aback by my outburst.

"Because in this world," I replied, "you don't live with us – you live here in Cambridge."

"Is that the only difference...?" Professor P began.

"But, Professor P!" I burst out. "It makes all the difference! You were our friend. We used to come and visit you almost every day. You were helping us to build a metal detector…"

"We'd really, really miss you and Sleepy," Tara added quietly.

"And that's why you want to return to your own world?" he asked slowly. "Because of me?"

"Yes," we said together.

Professor P paused. "Well, thank you," he said, slightly embarrassed. "I'm very touched by your feelings and I will do my very best to help you. First, I'll need to examine the time machine. Did you bring it with you?"

"No," I replied, "it crashed on the cliffs and the tubes smashed."

"What about the notebook computer?" he asked.

"I think it's still up on the cliffs too," I answered.

"Well, if I'm to have any chance of fixing the time machine," he said thoughtfully, "I'll have to examine the software on the computer. We'll need to recover it as soon as possible – I could come tomorrow if that's all right with you."

"Oh, yes, that would be great!" Tara and I cried together.

The waitress brought our sandwiches, drinks and cakes. As we ate lunch Professor P asked us more about our world. He laughed as we told him about his inventions and listened with great interest when we described Floppy.

"He must be a quantum computer," Professor P exclaimed. "Years ahead of anything that's been developed so far!"

When we finished our lunch Mary looked at her watch.

"It's almost three o'clock," she said. "I'm afraid we have to leave now, if we're going to get back home before dark."

Professor P paid the waitress and we all walked back to the car park together.

"Thank you for lunch, Professor P," Mary said, smiling

as we reached her car. She kissed him on the cheek and he blushed.

"Yes, thanks, Professor P," I said as we got into the car.

"It's been great to see you again," Tara added.

"Oh, the pleasure's been all mine," he replied, patting Sleepy on the head fondly.

"See you tomorrow," I called as the car pulled away.

CHAPTER TWENTY FOUR

Cliff Hanger

I jumped out of bed early the next day, feeling very excited about seeing Professor P again. I unplugged Floppy's sphere from the charger and he popped up as a white rabbit.

"What, what's been going on," he said, scratching his head. "Did you find Professor P?"

"Yes," I replied. "We went to Cambridge yesterday. Sorry I forgot to take you with us, Floppy. But everything went brilliantly! Professor P's coming to see us today!"

"He's coming here today!" Floppy cried. "That's wonderful news. I'm so looking forward to seeing him again."

Floppy changed into an owl and flew around the room, squawking excitedly.

"I'll wear my best clothes to greet him," he said, appearing in a black waistcoat with a large blue bow tie. "I must tell him my Theories of Everything, he'll be so impressed!"

"Professor P said he'd arrive at Mary's shop about eleven o'clock," I said, glancing at my watch. "Let's go and get Tara first."

I put Floppy's sphere into my pocket, called to Sparky and went downstairs. It was raining hard so I grabbed my raincoat and we dashed round to Tara house.

"You're soaking, Peter!" she said, opening the door.

"I do hope this rain stops soon!" I said as we went up to Tara's room.

"Me too," Tara said. "We won't be able to get the time machine if it doesn't. Oh, did you remember to bring Floppy?"

"He did," Floppy chirped up. "At you service!" he

added, bowing. Tara laughed.

We waited in Tara's room, glancing impatiently out of the window every few minutes, hoping the rain would stop. By quarter to eleven the rain clouds began to blow away and the sky cleared. When the rain had gone we rushed out of the house and ran all the way to the Fossil Shop.

"Hi," Mary greeted us cheerfully when we arrived. "That was good timing! Professor P just rang. He's on his way, he'll be here very soon."

A few minutes later a large white van with the words *Cambridge University Physics Department* painted on the side pulled up outside the shop. The van door opened and Sleepy jumped out, barking madly, delighted to see us again. Professor P jumped down from the van and greeted us with a broad smile.

"Welcome to my Fossil Shop, Professor P," Mary said as we went inside.

"Oh, this is lovely!" he commented, looking round at the displays. "You have some very interesting specimens here!"

"Thank you," she replied proudly.

"Professor P," I said, reaching into my pocket. "I remembered to bring Floppy this time."

I took out the small silver sphere and gave it to Professor P.

"So small?" he remarked as he examined the sphere closely.

"Tap it twice," Tara said. "And Floppy will appear."

Professor P tapped the sphere. There was a popping sound and Floppy appeared as a grey fluffy owl dressed in a black diner jacket. Professor P jumped back in surprise.

"Professor P," Floppy cried, his eyes lighting up. "How wonderful to see you again!"

"Hello, Floppy," Professor P said, looking at him curiously. "I am delighted to meet you."

"It's been so long..." Floppy began, "I don't know where to begin...I've been wanting to tell you about my Theories."

"Have you indeed?" Professor P said with interest.

"Yes," Floppy replied. "Would you like to hear my First Theory of Everything?

"I would," he replied.

Floppy flapped his wings and coughed once. "This is my First Theory of Everything." He paused for effect and then continued, "I think therefore."

Professor P looked uncertainly at Floppy for a moment. Then he smiled.

"Brilliant!" he said, his blue eyes twinkling with mirth. "Absolutely brilliant! Humorous, yet deep and profound. "

"Thank you, Professor P," Floppy said, blushing. "Would you like to hear my other theories?"

"I would love to, Floppy," he replied, glancing out of the window at the darkening sky. "But I think we need to get the time machine before it starts raining again."

We said goodbye to Mary and went outside to Professor P's van. He opened the back door and took out a large black bag. He heaved it onto his shoulder and we set off for the cliffs. Sleepy and Sparky ran on ahead and Floppy flew after them. We went through the village towards the beach and then up the footpath to the cliffs.

At the top of the hill we stopped to catch our breaths. A thick mist covered the sea and I could see no sign of the time machine. We continued walking and after a few minutes Floppy flew over excitedly. "The time machine!" he cried. "It's over there!"

Tara and I ran over to the cliff edge to look for it.

"Careful!" Professor P called out anxiously.

"It's all right," Tara said as we knelt down and leaned over the edge. "I can see it!"

We were directly above the time machine. It was caught

on a small ledge about ten metres below us. Professor P called to Sleepy and put her on the lead. They stayed on the footpath, keeping a safe distance from the edge, and then came over to us. I put Sparky on his lead too and we waited for them to join us.

Professor P took the large black bag off his shoulder. He opened it and Tara and I peered inside. All we could see was a jumble of ropes and metal fastenings.

"What is it?" I asked.

"Climbing equipment," Professor P explained. "I borrowed it from a friend in the University mountaineering club."

He took out the harness and fitted it around his waist and shoulders. He pulled out a coil of rope and we went over to the edge of the cliff.

"It's right there," I said, pointing to the time machine.

Professor P looked down and then walked rapidly away from the edge.

"Oh, dear," he said shakily.

"What is it, Professor P?" Tara asked.

"I, I..." he stammered, his face very pale, "I forgot I didn't like heights."

He sat down abruptly on the grass. Sleepy nuzzled him gently.

"Are you all right, Professor P?" I asked, concerned.

"No," he said. "I feel sick. I'm afraid I don't think I can go over the cliff edge."

"I'll go!" I said eagerly. "I did abseiling on holiday last Easter."

"Are you sure, Peter?" he asked doubtfully.

"Yes, I'll be fine," I insisted.

"I'll help," Floppy cried, perching on my shoulder.

I got into the harness and attached the rope to it. We hammered a stake deep into the ground, tied another piece of rope to it and joined the two sections of rope with a metal fastener. I put an empty rucksack on my back for the time machine and walked over to the edge of the cliff. I turned to face the cliff, leaned back against the rope and stepped slowly backwards.

"You're right on the edge now, Peter!" Floppy cried.

"Remember to bend your knees, Peter," Professor P called out, "and lean back away from the rope."

The ground was very slippery. I felt my stomach tense. This was not at all like the abseiling I had done on holiday. There was no wooden platform to stand on and no qualified instructor to help. As I looked down I saw the sharp rocks below and suddenly felt very dizzy.

"You're doing fine, Peter," Tara said encouragingly, reaching out a hand to support me.

"Thanks, Tara," I whispered. I stepped backwards carefully.

I placed my foot firmly onto the side of the cliff. I was over the edge now! I could do it!

I took another step down and another. A sudden gust of wind knocked me to one side and my foot slipped. The rope broke my fall and jerked me back abruptly. I hung from the rope, twisting uselessly in the air.

"Peter!" Floppy screeched.

I kicked against the cliff face, spun round and just managed to get a foothold in the cliff. I leaned back against the rope and caught my breath.

"Are you all right?" Tara cried as she peered over the edge of the cliff.

"I'm OK," I replied, panting.

"Tara, get away from there!" Professor P shouted. "Oh, this is far too dangerous! Come back, Peter. I'll pull you up."

"No, it's OK, Professor P," I called out. "I'm over the edge now, I'll be all right."

I waited a moment for the wind to die down and then

and took another step down the cliff.

"Let out more rope," I called to Professor P.

I gradually felt my way down the cliff until I was just above the ledge where the pyramid was lodged.

"You're almost there now, Peter!" Floppy cried.

I carefully stepped onto a narrow rocky platform.

"I made it!" I yelled, "I'm on the ledge!"

"Well done, Peter!" Professor P called down.

I steadied myself and then carefully picked up the notebook computer. It was

covered in mud and had scratches and dents in the case. I wiped it clean and put it into the rucksack. Most of the tubes from the time machine had cracked and the yellow fluid leaked out. I looked around and found one that was almost undamaged. I carefully wrapped it up in bubble wrap and put it into one of the side pockets of the rucksack.

"Pull me up!" I shouted excitedly. "I've got it!"

I went up the cliff slowly and carefully. As I neared the edge, Tara reached down to give me a hand.

"Your leg's bleeding!" she cried. "Are you all right?"

"It's only a scratch," I replied, rubbing my shin.

"Well done, Peter!" Professor P cried, taking my arm. "You did it!"

We walked away from the cliff edge and Professor P took the notebook computer out of the rucksack. Water dripped out of the case. He switched it on. Nothing happened.

"Looks as though the rain's shorted it out," he said.

"Can you fix it?" Floppy asked anxiously.

Professor P nodded, "I'll take out the hard drive and transfer the software to my own computer when I get back to Cambridge."

The rain started again and so we hurried back to Mary's shop. Professor P put the climbing equipment and the remains of the time machine in his van.

"Well, I'd better get back now, then I can start work on it straight away," he said, getting into the van.

"Oh, can't you stay for lunch?" Mary asked. "You've only just got here and it's such a long journey back to Cambridge. You're most welcome to come back to my house, all of you, it's only a few miles away."

"Thank you," Professor P said, smiling. "That's very kind of you."

Tara and I went in the car with Mary, while Sleepy and Sparky went in the van with Professor P. After a short drive through the winding lanes we arrived at a pretty little cottage with a very colourful and tidy garden.

"What a beautiful cottage, Mary!" Professor P commented as we went inside.

We walked through the house into the kitchen and sat at the table by the window overlooking a small orchard. Mary went over to the fridge and returned with a plate of sandwiches and a bowl of salad. Floppy turned into a rabbit and sat on the table, chewing a carrot!

"Professor P, how long will it take to fix the time machine?" I asked, reaching for a sandwich.

"I'm not sure," he replied. "Yesterday evening after you had left, I searched the Internet for scientific papers on alternative worlds."

"Did you find anything?" I asked, with interest.

"Oh, yes, lots," he replied. "As long ago as 1957 a

201

scientist called Hugh Everett published a paper on the Many Worlds Interpretation of Quantum Mechanics. It's an incredible theory!"

"What does it say?" I asked curiously.

He paused and then said. "What do you want to be when you grow up, Peter?"

"An inventor," I replied, unsure what this had to do with Quantum Mechanics. "Or a writer," I added.

"And what about you, Tara?" Professor P asked.

"I'd like to be an artist," she replied.

"I want to be a philosopher," Floppy said.

Professor P laughed. "You already are, Floppy!"

"Why do you ask, Professor P?" I said.

"Suppose I fix the time machine," he replied, "go twenty years into the future, have a look round and then return to the present. When I get back I could tell you both what your futures will hold. I could say 'Tara, you will be an artist and Peter, you will be a writer.'"

"Great!" I said happily.

"But would you really want that?" Professor P asked. "You wouldn't have any choice about your future – it would be decided for you."

"That's true," Tara said thoughtfully. "We'd know what was going to happen."

"Exactly," he nodded, "if there was only one future then you wouldn't have any freedom to choose your life. But suppose there wasn't just one future – suppose when I get in my time machine I can go to a world where Peter has become an inventor and Tara is a teacher – or a different world where you're both famous authors! That's what the alternative worlds are – they contain all the possible things that can happen."

I looked at Professor P in astonishment. "Are these worlds real?"

"Nothing is real," Floppy interrupted, taking the carrot

out of his mouth. "That's my Second Theory of Everything…"

"But do these alternative worlds really exist?" I interrupted.

"Absolutely," Professor P replied. "There's an infinite number of them, all as 'real' as this one! They all occupy the same space – they're all around us, but you can only see the one you're in, the others are invisible."

"So the world we came from is still here," Tara said, looking around in surprise, "but we just can't see it?"

"Yes, that's right," he replied.

"So when we came back from the Jurassic, why did we end up in the wrong world?" I asked.

"To be honest," Professor P replied, "I don't know. And I've also been wondering why in your world I moved away from Cambridge." He paused thoughtfully, "It's a complete mystery to me!"

CHAPTER TWENTY FIVE

The Exhibition

We finished lunch and after saying goodbye to Professor P, Sleepy and Floppy, Tara and I helped Mary with the washing up.

"I've been thinking about those beautiful ammonite shells you brought back from the past," Mary said as she was putting away the plates, "and I was wondering if you'd like to display them in my shop. Perhaps we could make a little exhibition in the back room."

"That's a great idea!" I said enthusiastically and Tara agreed.

"We could display my ichthyosaurus fossil too," Mary continued, "and some of my best ammonite fossils."

"We could make some really good posters of our prehistoric island!" Tara said. "I'd love to draw them."

"And I could write about all the plants and animals we saw," I added.

"Excellent!" Mary said, smiling. "We could call our exhibition *Life in the Jurassic*."

We finished in the kitchen and got into Mary's car to go home. On the journey we talked excitedly about our plans for the exhibition.

"We could make a little booklet to go with the exhibition," I suggested, "a fossil guide."

"What a good idea, Peter!" Mary said. "It would be nice for the visitors to have something to take away to remember what they've seen the exhibition."

"Can we have an opening party and invite all our friends?" Tara asked.

Mary smiled. "OK," she replied, "we'll have a grand launch party! What about next Saturday, that gives us all this week to get ready."

The car turned into our estate and we stopped outside my house.

"We'll start work on the displays straight away," I said as I got out of the car.

"Wonderful," Mary replied. "I'll clear out the back room this afternoon. Why don't you come over tomorrow and show me what you've done?"

"OK, see you tomorrow, Mary," we called, waving goodbye as she drove away.

Tara ran home to get her sketchpad and then we went up to my room. We talked about what we could put in the exhibition and began to rough out some ideas on paper.

"Let's do one really big picture of our island," Tara suggested, "with pterodactyls flying overhead, and ichthyosaurs swimming in the water…"

"And those seal-like animals on the beach," I added, "and a dinosaur coming out of the trees!"

"We can do some smaller detailed pictures of all the plants and animals as well," Tara continued. "We could show the ammonites…"

"And what about those strange dark green plants with the rubbery leaves," I said, "and those insects, the ones that looked like dragonflies…"

Tara picked up her pencil and began drawing. I watched in wonder as her hand flew over the paper and a pterodactyl appeared. She gave me the sketch and I coloured it in as she started on the next one.

"Can you remember what all the sea creatures looked like?" Tara asked.

"I'll never forget those sharks!" I replied. "And that huge shark-eater!"

Tara gave me the pencil and I did a rough sketch of the liopleurodon leaping out of the water with the shark in its mouth.

"You must have been terrified when you saw it," she said as she made a few improvements to make it look more realistic.

"It was pretty scary," I admitted, "but it was all over so quickly. It just burst out of the water and then disappeared back into the sea. I was more afraid of the sharks."

As Tara was drawing the island I wrote a few paragraphs describing how it felt to be there – the heat, the smells and the cries of the pterodactyls.

"I'd better not mention the tree house," I said, smiling.

"No," Tara chuckled, "but maybe one day someone will dig up its fossilised remains!"

"And decide that the dinosaurs were the first to invent *Superfoam*!" I laughed.

After a hurried tea I typed up the description of the island on my computer while Tara made labels for the exhibits with her calligraphy pens. At ten o'clock we had finished! We laid out all our posters on the floor and stood back to admire them.

"They're fantastic," I said, gazing at the pictures. Tara nodded.

We stood in silence for a few moments and remembered our amazing adventure on the prehistoric island.

Tara came round early the next morning. We carefully collected all our work and set off with Sparky for the village. When we arrived at the Fossil Shop we eagerly showed Mary what we had done.

"These are beautiful!" she exclaimed, looking at the pictures.

"Thanks, Mary," we said, beaming with pride.

"Oh, I wish I'd been there with you," she added after reading our description of the island. "It sounds incredible."

"It was," we replied together.

When Mary had finished looking at our work she took

us into the back room of the shop. She had already cleared and cleaned it but the paintwork was old and flaking away.

"The room needs completely redecorating," Mary said, "Let's go to the shops and buy some paint."

When we returned from the DIY store Tara and I sanded down the old woodwork while Mary filled the holes in the walls. We started painting after lunch. Sparky decided to help! He dipped his paw into the paint pot and left paw marks all over the floor!

By the end of the day the room was finished. The sun streamed through the window onto the peach coloured walls and gave them a soft warm glow.

"The room seems bigger now," Tara said as we admired our work.

"It certainly looks a lot more cheerful!" Mary added. "We've done a great job. When it's dry tomorrow we can start putting up the displays."

On our way home Tara and I decided to make the invitations that evening, so we could send them out in the morning post. She came round after tea and we sat down together at my computer to design the invitation cards.

"We must invite Professor P," she said, as the cards were printing.

"Good idea!" I replied. "I'll e-mail him tonight – it'll be quicker than posting an invitation."

"I do hope he can come!" she said. "It'll be great to see him again."

"And Sleepy too," I added, stroking Sparky as he lay at my feet.

"He might even have some news about the time machine," Tara said excitedly.

Before I went to bed I sent the e-mail to Professor P. As soon as I woke up in the morning I checked to see if he had replied.

"Yes!" I cried as the message appeared.

Dear Peter, thanks for your invitation, would love to come. I can't make it for the start but will be with you about 12 o'clock on Saturday.

See you then, love PP.

P.S. I have little present for you and Tara.

I got dressed and rushed round to Tara's house. She was delighted when I showed her Professor P's reply and we talked excitedly about what the *little present* could be.

After breakfast we walked to the Fossil Shop, chatting happily about seeing Professor P again. Mary was also very pleased when we told her he was coming to the party.

We all went into the back room and discussed how we could best arrange the exhibits. We decided to make the ammonite display first. Mary had found an old wooden cabinet with a glass top, which we cleaned and polished. When we had finished it shone and sparkled like new. We put it onto a table and placed it in the centre of the room. At the bottom of the cabinet we made a bed of fine white sand for the ammonites.

"Do you remember when we found these shells?" Tara asked as we arranged them neatly in their new home.

"Yes," I said, laughing, "and do you remember Floppy in that silly swimming costume!"

"Oh, he was great fun, wasn't he?" she said, smiling.

After a short break for lunch we started to put the posters on the walls. We fitted our large island picture into a glass frame and hung it on the wall opposite the window. We put Mary's large ichthyosaurus fossil next to it and then stuck the rest of our pictures and descriptions on the walls.

By the end of the day we had finished.

"It looks fabulous!" Mary exclaimed as she looked around at all the exhibits.

"Everyone will be really impressed!" Tara said proudly and I nodded in agreement.

"I'd rather not make a charge for the exhibition," Mary said as we walked into the shop. "But perhaps we could have a box for people to put donations in. We could give the money to a local charity. What do you think?"

Tara and I agreed it was a good idea.

"You could keep all the money you make from selling the fossil guides though," she added.

"Thanks, Mary," we said happily.

We left the shop and rushed home to start work on the fossil guide. I wrote down our ideas in my notebook as we talked. We wanted to include the most common fossils that could be found on the Jurassic Coast and we decided to have a sketch of each fossil alongside a drawing of what the animal looked like when it was alive.

We spent the rest of the week working hard on the fossil guide. We started by going to the library and borrowing all their fossil books. Then we went on the Internet and printed out as many interesting fossil facts as we could find. When we had gathered all the information we started to write the guide and lay it out on my computer.

It was late Friday evening when we finally finished. We printed out thirty copies of the fossil guide, neatly folded them and stapled the pages together.

"It's a great front cover," I said, admiring the border Tara had drawn around the front page.

"Thanks," she replied modestly.

After saying goodbye to Tara, I sat down exhausted on my bed. Sparky jumped up onto my lap and I stroked him gently.

"Professor P and Sleepy are coming!" I said, looking into his soft brown eyes.

"Woof," he barked, jumping off the bed and running excitedly over to the door.

"No, not now!" I laughed. "They're coming tomorrow!"

CHAPTER TWENTY SIX

Party!

It was Saturday – the day of our exhibition party! I jumped out of bed and after a hurried breakfast Sparky and I went to pick up Tara. We all raced down to the Fossil Shop.

"Hi, Peter, hi, Tara!" Mary said with a smile as we burst into the shop. "All ready for the big day?"

"Yes!" we replied breathlessly.

"Everyone should be arriving in a few hours," she continued, glancing at her watch. "I bought a few snacks and drinks and I was just going to put them out."

"Is there anything we can do?" I asked eagerly.

"Perhaps you could put up this banner I made, " Mary replied, "and blow up some balloons."

Tara and I started on the balloons. Sparky had never seen a balloon before and decided they were fun to chase around the shop. He finally cornered one and jumped on it. When it burst he scurried out of the shop, barking. A moment later he returned to pounce on another one!

As he played Tara and I hung some of the balloons inside the shop and the rest outside on the door. We tied the banner Mary had made across the window. It said *Life in the Jurassic – An Exhibition* in large black letters.

"It looks great!" I said, standing back to admire the banner.

We finished all our jobs just before eleven o'clock and waited inside the shop for our first visitors.

Everyone arrived at once! My parents, Tara's parents and her little sister Rosie, some of Tara's school friends, and a large group of Mary's friends, all piled into the Fossil Shop together. Mary served the drinks and then everybody went in to see the exhibition.

I glanced at Tara nervously as we went into the back room. What would they all think? Would they like it? It wasn't long before I heard the comments.

"It's wonderful!"

"Very impressive indeed."

"Beautiful drawings…"

"A marvellous job…"

Everyone wanted to talk to us at once and congratulate us on our displays.

Mary introduced us to a tall man wearing glasses. "Peter, Tara, I'd like you to meet a good friend of mine, Dr Edwards," she said. "He teaches geology at my old University."

"What a marvellous exhibition!" he said. "Your descriptions and drawings are all so realistic – I could almost believe you'd actually been there!"

"Thanks," I said, winking knowingly at Tara.

"You've also made an excellent fossil guide," he added, "I'd like to buy a few copies to take back with me to the department."

"Thank you," we said proudly.

We had a brilliant time showing our visitors around the exhibition and answering their questions. When everyone had asked all they wanted to know, Tara and I took a break and went into the main part of the shop. I looked at my watch. It was nearly twelve o'clock.

"Professor P will be here soon!" I said excitedly.

A few minutes later a white van pulled up in front of the shop. Tara and I dashed outside. The door opened and Sleepy jumped out, wagging her tail and running around madly. Sparky barked with joy when he saw her.

Professor P stepped out of the van. Tara and I ran over to give him a hug.

"Tara, Peter," he greeted us with a warm smile.

"Professor P!" I said happily. "It's really good to see

you again!"

"I'm so glad you could come to our exhibition," Tara added.

"I wouldn't have missed it for the world!" he replied.

Floppy flew out of the van as a brightly coloured parrot and perched on Professor P's shoulder.

"Hi, Floppy," I smiled. "You look great!"

"Thanks," he squawked.

We went into the shop and Mary came over to say hello and offer Professor P a drink.

"I didn't know you had a parrot, Professor P," she said, looking curiously at the bright green and red bird perched on his shoulder.

To Mary's great surprise, the parrot spoke. "Hello, Mary," it squawked.

Tara giggled.

"Oh, Floppy!" Mary laughed. "I didn't realise it was you!"

We all went into the exhibition room and Professor P walked around the exhibits slowly. He looked at our drawings and carefully read all the descriptions we had written.

"You've made an excellent exhibition!" he said when he had finished looking at everything.

"Thanks, Professor P," we said, pleased.

"I just wish I'd been there with you!" he whispered with a twinkle in his eye.

"Don't forget to give Peter and Tara your *little present*!" Floppy said quietly into Professor P's ear.

"Oh, yes, of course," he said, reaching into his jacket pocket. He took out a large envelope.

"Is there somewhere private we could go?" he asked mysteriously.

Mary led us out into a small courtyard at the back of the shop. Professor P closed the door firmly behind us then gave us the envelope. We opened it eagerly, curious to know what was inside.

I gasped in amazement.

"Photos!" I cried. "Photos of our prehistoric island!"

"But…but how?" Tara asked. "How did you get them?"

"Professor P downloaded them from my memory," Floppy explained proudly.

"Our tree house!" Tara exclaimed as we leafed through the photos. "Oh, thank you!" she added tearfully. "I thought we'd never see it again."

"I thought you'd like them," Professor P said, smiling.

By one o'clock all the visitors to the exhibition had left and Mary closed the shop for lunch.

"Anyone for sandwiches?" she asked. "I could pop over to the baker's and we can eat them outside."

"Yes, please," we replied hungrily.

When Mary returned we all went into the courtyard and sat in the sun to eat.

"Have you had any success with the time machine yet, Professor P?" I asked.

"Yes, he replied. "I think I understand how it works and I've started to build a new one. Hopefully, I should have a working prototype in a few weeks."

"That's fantastic!" I cried. "So we'll be able to return to our own world soon."

"Well, that's not so easy…" he said, hesitating. "I'm afraid that may take much longer. The problem with getting you back is – how do I know exactly which alternative world you came from? It'll be a bit like finding a needle in a haystack!"

"Actually an infinitesimally small needle in an infinitely large haystack," Floppy added.

"Exactly, Floppy," Professor P nodded. "I'm afraid it is a very difficult problem indeed."

"How long do you think it will take?" I asked.

"I don't know exactly," Professor P replied. "It could be," he paused, "years…"

"Years!" I exclaimed.

"I'm afraid so," Professor P continued. "You see I don't want to risk sending you back to the wrong world. Some of the alternative worlds could be very dangerous places and I wouldn't like you to get trapped in one of them."

Professor P cleared his throat. "I don't know how you feel about this but …" he paused. "I think it would be best if you stayed in this world and didn't risk using the time machine again."

I did not know what to say. I was stunned by this unexpected news. I did not like the idea of using the time machine and getting trapped in a dangerous alternative world. But I did not want to live here without Professor P and Sleepy and Floppy. I looked at Tara. She was shocked by the news too.

"I'm sorry to bring you such bad news," Professor P said. "I only wish there was something I could do…"

"There is something you can do, Professor P!" I burst out. "You could move here. Then we won't need to go back to our old world and this world will be just like the one we left…"

"Oh, yes," Tara cried happily, "You'll love living here, Professor P, you could be an inventor again and…"

She stopped as she saw the look on Professor P's face.

"I'm sorry," he said solemnly. "But my work is in Cambridge. I have an excellent job and…"

"But, Professor P," Floppy piped up. "I think Peter and Tara are right. You were very happy when you lived here."

"We had such a great time," I added. "And you loved being an inventor, Professor P. You invented the most amazing things, and they were really fun!"

"You even invented chocolate flavoured crisps," Tara added, "and balls that wouldn't stop bouncing. Do you remember them, Peter."

"I'll never forget!" I said, rubbing my head.

"And you had a *very* special safe, Professor P!" Tara said, grinning.

"Did I indeed?" he said interestedly.

"Yes," I chuckled. "It exploded if you got the combination wrong. It gave us quite a shock when we tried to open it!"

"I think just about everything in your house did something unusual!" Tara said thoughtfully.

"You also invented me, Professor P," Floppy said quietly.

Professor P looked at Floppy and smiled. "I'm very proud of that, Floppy. You're very special."

"Thank you," he said, blushing.

"Sleepy loved it here too, Professor P," I said, patting her on the head.

"It certainly is a very beautiful place to live," Mary added. "I'm very glad that I moved here."

Tara jumped up. "Let's go down to the beach, Professor P – we'll show you around and you'll see how nice it is."

Sleepy ran over to the door. She wagged her tail excitedly and looked pleadingly at Professor P.

"All right," he laughed. "Come on, Sleepy!"

We thanked Mary for lunch and set off for the beach. Sparky and Sleepy ran ahead of us as we walked through the village.

"We found some great fossils over there, Professor P," Tara said, pointing to the cliffs. "We used to have great fun looking for them together."

"And gold too," I said.

"Gold!" Professor P exclaimed in surprise.

"Well, not real gold," I explained. "It's called fool's gold, but it looks just like the real thing."

Professor P smiled. We continued along the beach and

he chuckled merrily as we told him about more of his funny inventions.

"But they weren't all just for fun," I said. "You invented a solar-powered kettle that made dirty water safe for drinking."

"You said it could save lives in third world countries," Tara added.

"Now that is a good idea," Professor P said.

When we came to the steps in the cliff we raced up them two at a time and then stopped at the top to catch our breaths.

"What a beautiful view," Professor P said as he gazed out to sea.

"See that island over there?" I said, pointing excitedly. "It wasn't there in our world."

"Really?" he said curiously.

"We want to go there," Tara added, "and build a tree house, just like the one on our prehistoric island!"

"You could help us, Professor P."

Professor P laughed. "Well, I suppose you will need some of my *Superstuff*! Now, I wonder how I made that…"

Sleepy barked and ran off along the footpath down towards Professor P's old cottage. Sparky happily chased after her.

"Come back, Sleepy," Professor P called out to her. "Oh, where is she going?"

"I think she's going home," I replied. "That's where you used to live, Professor P. In a cottage just through those woods."

He looked curiously at the trees.

"Would you like to see your old house?" Tara asked.

"Why not?" he replied, smiling. "It won't harm to have a look!"

We followed Sparky and Sleepy down the footpath and through the trees to the cottage.

When we reached the gate I stopped and stared in amazement at a sign in the front garden.

"Professor P!" I cried, hardly able to contain my excitement. "It's for sale!"

"Oh, Professor P, you can buy it!" Tara exclaimed.

Professor P stood and gazed at the cottage in silence. Then he turned to us and smiled.

THE END?

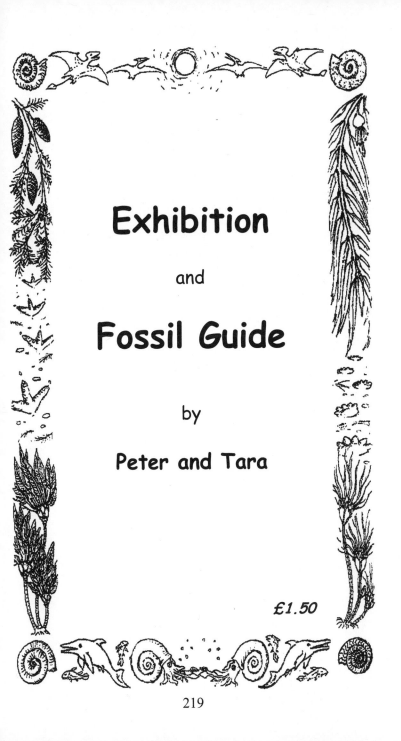

Exhibition

and

Fossil Guide

by

Peter and Tara

£1.50

Welcome to our exhibition

We really hope you enjoy visiting our fossil exhibition. All the fossils on display were found here on the Jurassic Coast. This little guide will show you what fossils were like when they were alive, give you tips on how to find them and tell you all sorts of interesting things.

We would like to thank everyone who has helped us make the exhibition and this fossil guide, especially Mary for allowing us to use her shop and lending us her Ichthyosaurus fossil, and of course Professor P. With him the exhibition would never have been possible!

Best wishes,

Peter & Tara

What is a fossil?

A fossil is the remains of a plant or animal that lived a long time ago. Usually only the hard parts of the animal such as the shell, teeth or bones become fossilised.

When creatures die they fall to the sea floor and the soft parts rot away. The bones become covered in mud.

Over millions of years the mud turns into rock and the bones are replaced by minerals.

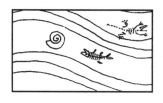

Many more millions of years later the rocks are folded by the earth's movements.

Eventually the rocks are eroded away to expose the fossils.

Geological time scales

According to scientists, the earth was formed about 4,500 million years ago and the earliest fossil life is believed to be 3,400 millions of years old. Dinosaurs appeared 250 million years ago at the beginning of the Triassic Period and died out 65 million years ago at the end of the Cretaceous Period. They were probably destroyed when a giant asteroid hit the earth.

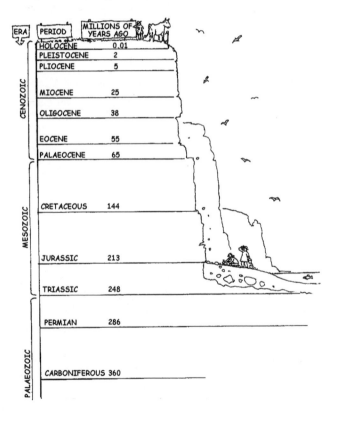

ERA	PERIOD	MILLIONS OF YEARS AGO
CENOZOIC	HOLOCENE	0.01
	PLEISTOCENE	2
	PLIOCENE	5
	MIOCENE	25
	OLIGOCENE	38
	EOCENE	55
	PALAEOCENE	65
MESOZOIC	CRETACEOUS	144
	JURASSIC	213
	TRIASSIC	248
PALAEOZOIC	PERMIAN	286
	CARBONIFEROUS	360

Finding fossils

There are many great places to find fossils in Britain. The fossil-bearing rocks are often covered with topsoil so quarries and on the coast are the best places to look.

The Jurassic Coast World Heritage Site

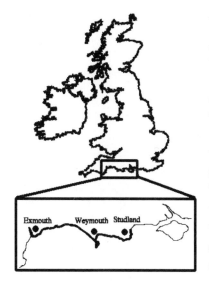

You can take a journey back in time, from Studland in Dorset where the rocks are 65 million years old to Exmouth in East Devon where the rocks are 250 million years old. There are some good fossils to be found on the beach, especially at Lyme Regis and Charmouth.

SAFETY FIRST!

Don't climb the cliffs!
Don't collect fossils from the cliffs!
Keep away from the cliff edges!
Always use the proper equipment!
Always check the tides!

Ammonites

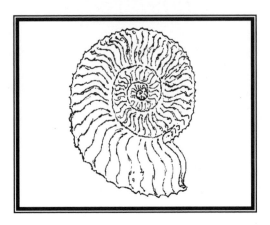

Ammonite fossil

What, where & when?

Ammonites were sea creatures that lived during the Jurassic and Cretaceous Periods. They died out 65 million years ago at the time of the mass extinction.

Ammonite dating

Geologist use ammonites to help them find out how old rocks are. They can do this because different species of ammonites lived at different times during the Jurassic Period.

Did you know?
Ammonites were once called snake-stones and were thought to possess magical powers.

Ammonites

Living ammonite – artist's impression

Jet propulsion

Ammonites propelled themselves by squirting water through a muscular tube called the siphon. They had suckered tentacles and kept themselves afloat with gas-filled chambers.

Cephalopods

Ammonites belong to the family of animals called cephalopods. They are similar to squid and octopi but have external shells.

Did you know?

The Nautilus is a very similar creature to the ammonite and can still be found living in the depths of the Pacific Ocean.

Belemnites

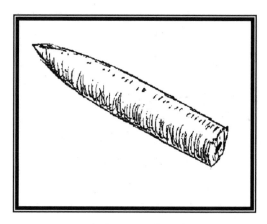

Belemnite fossil

What, where & when?

Belemnites were very common in the Jurassic and Cretaceous Periods and a few species survived until about 40 million years ago.

The guard

Belemnites were squid-like creatures with a hard internal shell known as the guard. In most fossils only the bullet-shaped guard remains but in well-preserved fossils the soft part of the body can still be seen.

Did you know?

Belemnites used to be called St Peter's Fingers and were believed to have healing powers. Powdered belemnite was used to cure infections in horses' eyes.

Belemnites

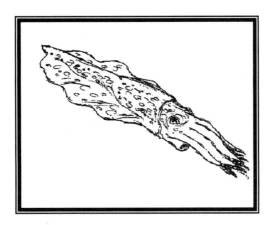

Living Belemnite – artist's impression

Fast food

They were active predators, moving quickly through the water using jet propulsion. They ate small fish and crustaceans.

Ten tentacles

Like squids, Belemnites had ten tentacles, an ink sack and large well-developed eyes. The hard internal shell, made of calcite, was used to help balance the animal in water and improve stability while swimming.

Did you know?
The largest modern squid on record is 19 metres long.

Crinoids

Crinoid fossil

What, where & when?

Crinoids belong to the group of animals known as Echinoderms, which includes sea urchins and starfish. They were very common in the Jurassic Period and although rare now, can still be found in the Pacific Ocean.

Five fold symmetry

Crinoids attach themselves to the seabed with long jointed stems. Each segment of the stem looks like a tiny starfish. They feed on small particles of food, which they waft towards their mouths by swaying their arms.

Crinoids

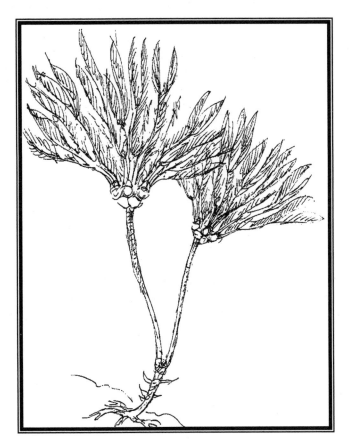

Living crinoid

Did you know?
Crinoids look so much like plants they are often called sea lilies.

Ichthyosaurs

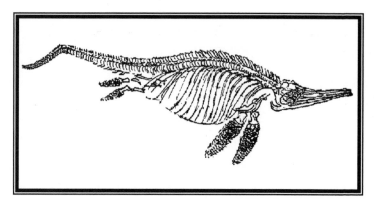

Ichthyosaurs fossil

What, where & when?

Although they look very like dolphins they are not a related species. Ichthyosaurs were cold-blooded reptiles, more similar to crocodiles. They were alive in the Jurassic and died out at the end of the Cretaceous Period, 65 million years ago.

Fossil finds

It is rare to find a complete ichthyosaurus but teeth and bones, especially the vertebrae are often found. The bones are quite heavy, hard and glossy and can be black or brown in colour.

Did you know?

Ichthyosaurs are also known as Sea Dragons.

Ichthyosaurs

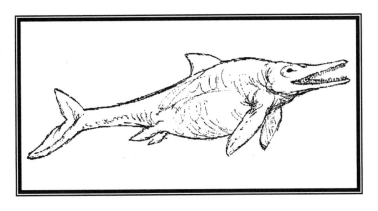

Living ichthyosaurus – artist's impression

Tough teeth

Ichthyosaurs had long jaws packed with short sharp teeth, ideal for crunching ammonites. They had large eyes and a streamlined body for fast swimming. They grew up to 10 metres in length.

Live young

When scientists first discovered small ichthyosaurus fossils inside larger ones they thought they were cannibals. Scientists now believe that ichthyosaurs, unlike most other reptiles, gave birth to live young.

Did you know?

In 1812 a 13 year old girl called Mary Anning found the first complete ichthyosaurus fossil and sold it for £23.

Plesiosaurs

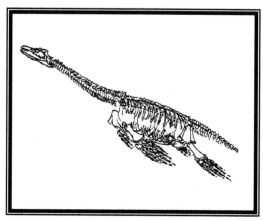

Plesiosaurus fossil

What, where & when?

Plesiosaurs were sea reptiles 3 to 8 metres in length with small heads and long necks. They were very common in the Jurassic and Cretaceous Periods and died out 65 million years ago.

Fossil bones

Plesiosaurus fossils are quite rare but loose vertebrae and flipper bones can sometimes be found.

Did you know?

In 1823 Mary Anning uncovered a complete fossil plesiosaurus three metres long. Scientists did not believe that any animal could have had such a long neck and accused her of faking it.

Plesiosaurs

Living plesiosaurus – artist's impression

Long neck

Plesiosaurs swam slowly through the sea, catching fish and ammonites by quickly moving their long necks. They breathed air and frequently came up to the surface to fill their lungs.

Sinking stones

Evidence suggests that plesiosaurs used to scrape up stones from the seabed and swallow them to help themselves dive.

Did you know?

Some people think that the Loch Ness Monster is a relative of the plesiosaur.

Sharks

Shark tooth fossil

Survivors

Sharks belong to a very old group of fish. Teeth have been found dating back 350 – 400 million years ago. Unlike other animals, sharks have changed very little since then.

Cold blooded

Sharks are cold blooded and breathe underwater through gills. Their nostrils are used for smell only; they have an amazing sense of smell and are able to detect one drop of blood in a million drops of water.

Did you know?

Teeth 15cm long have been found from a giant 15m relative of the modern Great White Shark.

Sharks

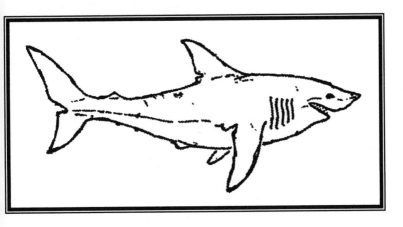

Modern great white shark

Shark teeth

Shark skeletons are soft and rarely become fossilised but you can find well-preserved fin spines and still sharp teeth.

Electricity

Sharks can detect electricity. They use the tiny electric currents that all living creatures produce to find their prey.

Did you know?

New shark teeth grow all the time, replacing the old ones as they fall out. Some species of shark may shed 30,000 teeth in their lifetime.

Professor P's website

Visit **www.ProfessorP.co.uk** for –

Deleted scenes

So many great scenes wouldn't fit into the book! But don't worry – they're all on the website. Here are some of my favourites -

Peter's birthday
Peter's father has just bought an expensive video camera for Peter's birthday party. Peter accidentally breaks it and when Professor P attempts to 'fix it' the consequences are hilarious!

Professor P's outdoor inventions
Peter and Tara have fun helping Professor P try out his latest range of outdoor inventions. There's his solar-powered kettle that works from sea-water, his electronic child-finder and other useful inventions!

Floppy meets Poppy
When Floppy meets an alternative version of himself he is very confused at first and sparks fly! Will they ever make friends?

Fun facts

Are you interested in science and inventing? Look on the website to discover how some of Professor P inventions work. Find out about –

Supercomputers
Will computers ever become as intelligent as people? How does a quantum computer work?

Time travel
Is it possible to build a time machine? Can you change the past and do alternative worlds really exist?

Fossils
Learn more about finding fossils and follow the links to some great Jurassic Coast and fossil sites.

Coming soon

Our interactive website will soon give you the chance to try out some exciting games –

Exploding safe
Try your hand at cracking Professor P's safe! Solve the clues to figure out the combination before your time is up.

Shark attack
Can you guide your raft through the shark-infested waters?

About Positive Books

We publish positive books that promote peace and non-violence. We are an ethical and green company and our books are printed on recycled paper.

Our books are available at your local bookstore or can be ordered directly from us.

Please send cheque/postal order (Sterling only) made payable to **Positive Books Limited** to:

> **Positive Books Limited**
> **66 High Street**
> **Glastonbury**
> **Somerset**
> **BA6 9DZ**

Or order online at:
www.positive-books.co.uk

Postage is free in the UK. Please add £2.00 per book for overseas. Please allow 28 days for delivery.

Prices and availability are subject to change without notice. When placing your order, please mention if you do not wish to receive further information.